SUBWAY

LOVE

SUBWAY

LOVE

NORA RALEIGH BASKIN

CANDLEWICK PRESS

Copyright © 2014 by Nora Raleigh Baskin

Chapter opener photograph appears courtesy of Error46146 at en.wikipedia (http://en.wikipedia.org).

First edition 2014

Library of Congress Catalog Card Number 2013946617
ISBN 978-0-7636-6845-7

14 15 16 17 18 19 BVG 10 9 8 7 6 5 4 3 2 1

Printed in Berryville, VA, U.S.A.

This book was typeset in Garamond.

Candlewick Press
99 Dover Street
Somerville, Massachusetts 02144

visit us at www.candlewick.com

This one is for Susan.

1

LAURA remembered the day it was taken, or rather she remembered as soon as she saw the photo, pinned to the folding display panel among all the others. It was a black-and-white picture of *her* sitting on a swing, clutching the chain in one hand, her eleven-year-old face smudged with dirt, and her blackened bare feet poking out from the bottom of frayed overalls. It was taken at the Sunday picnic in Woodstock on the town green, 1969, just three years earlier, and now here it was, for sale.

Laura didn't say anything. She just stared at herself in the photograph. The other photos, all mounted on the same gray-matte board, revealed scenes meant to capture the time, *this* hippie time that was already passing, that had already passed. The artist, at least Laura assumed he was the artist, didn't recognize her. He sat on his metal stool chatting with a prospective buyer.

One photo held the image of a young couple in a close embrace. The girl, or woman, or girl-woman, was wearing a long velvet dress with lace trimming the ends of the wide sleeves. If the picture were in color, the dress might have been red or deep purple, like velvet is meant to be. The man was shirtless, his skinny hip bones protruding from his jeans, and wisps of curly hair reaching out of his pants and up to his belly.

Laura turned her head away.

Another photo showed a wildly bearded man sitting on a milk crate, playing the guitar; the varnish was worn where his hand had moved up and down hundreds, if not thousands, of times across the strings. He was looking directly into the camera.

"Can I help you?" The photographer must have lost his sale. He was alone now, without a customer, and he turned his attention to Laura.

"Oh—no," Laura answered.

He still didn't seem to realize who she was; that an older version of this girl he was talking to hung on the board behind him, the actual in-the-flesh representative of the 1960s flower children that he was trying to peddle. What right had he to sell this picture, her image, her moment in time?

"You like my work," he said. He didn't ask.

Laura answered, "Not particularly."

She walked away from the man's booth. It was a huge crafts fair, and her mother had told her these kinds of massive events were going to be big in the future. Laura's mother said she could make a lot of money selling leather goods, headbands, vests, and fringed pocketbooks. Not that they wanted a lot of money. Just enough to live on. Anything more than that was being a Capitalist Pig.

According to her mother, those people (people like her father) were deluded and misguided. They were squares and they were conservatives. They were Republicans.

When she was in elementary school, Laura used to open her lunch, praying she could be a Republican, praying that there had been some horrible switch, some crack in the fabric of the universe that had dumped her into this life, and that right at this moment, she would slip back into reality, a reality that put a Skippy peanut butter and Welch's grape jelly sandwich on Wonder bread and a bottle of Yoo-hoo in front of her. If the universe really wanted to be nice, there might even be a Twinkie or a Hostess cupcake. Laura would watch her friends unroll their

Yodels and lick the white insides while she bit into her peanut butter (all-natural, unsalted, and awful), banana, and honey sandwich on cracked whole wheat.

"Hey, you," the photographer called after her. "Isn't this you?" He pointed to his own work. "It's you, isn't it? Just younger."

Laura looked at the picture once more, as if only just now considering the claim. She had dressed like her mother wanted that day; she ran around barefoot, holding out her hand and begging for food from the other picnickers (because, after all, wasn't Jesus a rebel, a long-haired freak who loved the poor?), playing the part of the carefree Woodstock flower child.

"No," Laura answered, "that's not me."

The man looked back and forth from Laura to the photograph. "No, it is. I remember now. You and your friend were taking turns on the swing. It was the end of the afternoon, in Woodstock. The Sunday picnic. It was bloody hot. I remember."

Laura shook her head. "Not me."

"Oh, yeah?" the man said. "Well, whatever you say, babe, but my work is important. You're too young to understand, but this is all going to end, and someday people will look back, and they won't have faith anymore; they won't remember. But I'll have the proof."

Laura wanted to tell him she *did* understand. She wanted to tell him what it was going to be like in the future, but she knew he wouldn't believe her.

JONAS'S cell phone dropped into the toilet again. It wasn't his fault, but of course, it was. It tipped off the toilet tank when he was getting out of the shower.

"Shit," he said out loud. He was already late for school. Twelve unexcused tardies meant a full-point drop in his GPA. Not that he cared. It was all a load of crap, but for some reason it bothered him. He stubbed his toe reaching for something to dry himself with. Dirty towels were scattered on the bathroom floor, too damp to use, along with a couple of pairs of underwear, stray socks.

"Shit." Why does a big toe hurt so damn much? You'd think it would be more resilient being out there on the front lines.

Worse, his Droid looked dead. He took out the battery, left the whole thing open on the sink, and hoped for a miracle.

"Jonas," his mother called up the stairs, "it's six fifty-six."

"Thanks for the info, Mom," Jonas said. If he ran

out of the apartment now, he might be lucky enough to jump directly onto the train, walk the five blocks to school, and make it there before they locked the doors. He'd have to be buzzed in then, a surefire tardy.

"Do you want breakfast?"

He hated those kinds of questions. Of course he wanted breakfast, but he was late, and even if he wolfed down a bowl of cereal as fast as he could, he'd be that much later. If he took time to tie his shoes, he'd be later still.

His mother was standing in the hall in her bathrobe, coffee in hand.

"I'll take some coffee," Jonas said. "To go."

His mother smiled widely, as if this was going to be the greatest accomplishment of her day. Being a person's be-all and end-all is a heavy load.

"Consider it done," she said. She handed him a thermos. "Light, no sugar."

It could have been his father's load too, but even before they split up, it wasn't.

"Thanks, Mom," Jonas said. He grabbed his army jacket and headed out.

Jonas missed the 6 train by two seconds, watched the doors closing—faces inside speeding away—and wondered if it was worth it going to school at all at this point.

2

CHANGE floated on four-four time from the apartment next door right into their window, and just like that, the world as Laura knew it began to unravel. It began long before they moved to Woodstock, before crafts fairs, before long hair, before any town picnic. It began when her parents were still married, when they all still lived in New York City. Laura was seven, her brother ten.

"It's so hot." Mitchell waved his hand in front of his face. He was sprawled on the couch in front of the television set. *Chiller Theater* was about to begin.

The windows were open wide, which never failed to elicit the same debate, whether it was hotter with the windows open or closed. Their mother couldn't stand the stuffiness. Their father said having the windows open just brought in hotter air from outside, but that day, it brought in music, a rhythmic guitar accompanying a whiny, pleading voice singing about a tambourine and a journey on a magical ship. Laura stood by the window, listening.

As always when a babysitter was coming over, Laura's parents were going out with the Hanssens, and so five kids — three Hanssens plus Laura and Mitchell — were dumped together in one apartment or the other. This time it was Laura and Mitchell's apartment, which is why Mitchell got the couch.

The grown-ups were busy chatting about the film they were about to see. Mitchell and John were arguing about who should get the prime real estate on the couch so he could stretch his legs. The two Hanssen sisters were clutching each other while the creepy six-fingered hand rose out of the ground and the deep, wavy voice announced the start of the show. Laura stood by the window and felt a secret kinship with the music no one else seemed interested in or even able to hear.

She didn't know exactly where the song was coming from, or who was singing. At that moment, Laura's mother walked into the living room wearing a plain sheath and flat shoes, with her hair in a neat bob — a veritable, fashionable, and very conservative take on Jackie Kennedy.

"Hey, sweetie," her mother said. "Why aren't you watching television with everyone else?" She ran her hand over Laura's head gently.

"I will," Laura answered. She turned away from the window. The episode was starting, "Attack of the 50 Foot Woman." She needed to find space for herself on the floor next to Julie or Lizzy Hanssen, far away from the boys.

Then Laura caught the look on her mother's face as she heard the song. The desperate, urging music that leaked randomly from someone's open window would somehow have the power to change all their lives, but no one knew it then.

Jonas sat down on the bench and waited for the next train. He might not be going to school, but he sure wasn't going back home. The platform was crowded with commuters, everyone vying for personal space: an angry businesswoman in a blue suit bumping into an earbudded kid in pants belted around his butt; a future famous movie star on her way to a waitress gig alongside a corporate ad executive who didn't lift his eyes from his BlackBerry. And they all had the same goal—to cram into the next train and get where they needed to be in as little time and with as little acknowledgment of one another as possible.

Jonas stayed seated, letting five trains come and go, watching hundreds of people pouring out and hundreds more getting sucked inside and being whisked away, and eventually the crowd thinned out altogether.

A pretty girl wearing those large headphones, the thick, padded kind that shut out the whole world, sat down next to him. She swayed ever so slightly to music that must have been thunderously loud, since the beat was audible three feet away. Jonas hadn't seen her walk over, so he had no way of determining how tall or short she was. He never tried talking to a girl who was taller than he was, no matter how pretty, and it seemed each year his choices were diminishing. Her audio technology precluded that from happening anyway. Maybe that was her point.

When the next train stopped, she got up and hopped on. Jonas could see her, silently dancing, as she held on to the metal pole inside. He smiled to himself. The doors hissed shut and the whole image was gone. Girls, or getting girls, had not been his strong suit, not since third grade, which he now considered the height of his romantic life, when he and James Michelson duked it out during recess to see who would get

Sabrina Branch to be his girlfriend. James pushed him twice, Jonas pushed him back once, before the playground monitor broke it up, giving them both detention, and by that time Sabrina had changed her mind about her potential relationship status.

"I don't want to be anyone's girlfriend," she announced, and she ran off to the basketball courts.

Last time he checked, Sabrina had updated herself as "in a relationship" with Caroline Fein and posted ridiculously provocative webcam photos of the two of them hugging and kissing. Photos had become so meaningless. Anyone could take one, anytime, anywhere, and everyone did, all the time. They took pictures with digital cameras, digital video cameras, with cell phones, with their computers. There was a picture of everything.

If 9/11 had happened today, there would be hundreds of videos, the more graphic the better, getting millions of hits all over YouTube. In fact, 9/11 was probably the last major event in human history not to be recorded, posted, tweeted, retweeted, and viewed over and over and over for all time.

Jonas preferred real photography, the kind that took skill and still had meaning, even if he had discovered it by accident. He had found the old film camera in the back of his parents' closet. His dad must have missed it, or left it on purpose, knowing it was useless, like, apparently, his family was. It was heavy, a Canon AE-1. When Jonas picked it up by its thin black strap, the whole thing tipped forward and he nearly banged it against the dresser. "Whoa."

"Jonas, what are you doing in there?" He could tell by Lily's thick mucusy voice that she had been crying, when the last thing he needed was more crying.

"Nothing. Go find Mom," he called out. He waited for the footsteps, but his sister didn't move. He could hear her breathing behind the closed bedroom door. "OK, Lily, come in. But shut the door behind you and be real quiet."

Lily had burst into the room, throwing herself down onto the carpet next to her brother. Jonas furrowed his brow at her.

"Oh, right." She jumped up and closed the door with a bang.

His sister was eight, six years younger than he was. She didn't understand what was happening. She kept asking when Daddy was coming home from the hospital.

"Lily," their mother would try to explain, "your daddy's been out of the hospital for weeks. It was just a kidney stone, sweetie. Daddy's fine. He lives in his own apartment now."

And Lily would answer with "Yeah, but when will he be home?"

She plopped back down on the floor next to her brother. "What's that?"

"A camera," Jonas told her. He turned it over in his hands. There was a long lens and lots of dials with tiny numbers. He clicked open the back, where the film would drop inside.

"Mommy's being mean to me. Again," Lily said.

"No, she's not, Lily. And I know you know Daddy moved out. We saw his new apartment last week. You can't get what you want just by wanting it bad enough."

Jonas watched Lily's eyes filling up. "Lily, I'm here. It's OK. It's going to be OK. Nobody stays married anymore. I mean, seriously, who do you know whose parents are married?"

He put down the camera and wrapped his arm around his sister. "And look on the bright side: We get double presents on our birthdays."

"Is that a present?" she asked.

Jonas picked up the camera again. "It is now," he said.

And he really hadn't gone many places without it since. Another train rolled to a stop at the platform and the doors flew open. It had been two years since his dad moved out. It took Jonas a moment to notice the smattering of loopy red lettering covering the side of the subway car. At first he thought it might be promotional graffiti, the kind in the shuttle trains when the Yankees won the World Series or the Rangers the Stanley Cup. But no, this didn't look commercial. It was just good old-fashioned messy graffiti.

You never saw that anymore in New York.

Maybe it was a MoMA retrospective: New York Subway Art, the Lost Era.

Of course, it would have been easier to flip open a phone, press the power button on a digital camera, point and click, and snap two or four or five pictures, but Jonas reached for his Canon AE-1. This meant unscrewing the lens cap, checking the light meter, twisting the aperture, and setting the shutter speed, and by the time he did all that, the subway was picking up speed. The photo would be blurry. It might not even be recognizable, but Jonas was pretty certain he had captured the image.

3

VISITING her dad was usually a good thing. This week they skipped school Friday and headed into New York first thing in the morning. Mitchell didn't care since he rarely went to school anyway, but Laura worried about what she was missing. Still, there was plenty to look forward to at her dad's, like eating.

The best part of being there would be the food. Or maybe it was getting to watch TV, since part of their mom's rejection of the Establishment was to get rid of the television set. When they moved from Brooklyn to Woodstock three years ago, neither her father nor the TV came with them.

The worst part was traveling on the bus from Kingston to Port Authority with her brother. It wasn't just the long bus ride; if Mitchell wasn't in a good mood, he would sit by himself, and when they got to the city, he would walk ahead, briskly. Laura needed to know her way around the New York subway system or keep up.

"Mitchell, wait for me," she said, mostly to her brother's backpack.

It was an army surplus bag that he wore over his shoulders. It matched his army surplus field jacket. Mitchell had sewn a peace-sign patch on the breast pocket, right over the original owner's name.

"Hurry up, then."

Laura quickened her step, trying to keep a slightly slower than running pace and managing a sort of half skip. Mitchell would make a show of it for their dad, looking like the good older brother, then within half an hour, he'd be hogging the television *and* the couch *and* the Chinese food, and making faces at her when their dad wasn't looking. It was as if he held his sister responsible for his fragmented travels back and forth every other weekend or so. Clearly he wished he could just stay home with their mom and her new boyfriend, Bruce, because when the winds of change swallowed up half the world, it took their mother with it, and

Mitchell followed more than willingly. It was now three against one.

Mitchell was heading down the steep steps underground, dodging people coming up and avoiding people who wanted to get quickly down. Laura was right behind him.

"Look, we just missed it," Mitchell said. The last car of the subway was pulled around the bend and was gone. The platform was empty. Mitchell plopped down on the wooden bench and let his legs stretch out in front, his feet balanced on the heel of his work boots. "Nice work, Laura."

Maybe if she wasn't so tired from the bus ride, or out of breath from running, she might have responded, but there wasn't much her brother didn't hold her responsible for. Laura saved her energy to concentrate on her surroundings. The fact that Mitchell was constantly high didn't exactly promote security. Best she stay alert.

Sometimes Laura tried to imagine her life had her parents not gotten divorced and had they all stayed in New York City. She'd be an urban kid, hopping subways, maybe jumping on the back of city buses and holding on for dear life. She had a vague memory of sitting in the last row of a crosstown bus with her mom, seeing the faces of daredevil teenagers hanging outside the rear window, staring in, laughing. Of course, a few short months later, her mother would have been exulting in their anticapitalist method of travel, but that day she just explained that the teenagers were avoiding the bus fare.

Laura figured that if her parents had stayed married, she'd know her way around the city without having to look up every block at each street sign and calculate the avenues. She probably wouldn't be afraid, the way she was now, in this dank underground that smelled like urine and was littered with garbage and graffiti. At least it was empty.

"I think I hear the train," Laura said. She took a look to each side and behind her, to make sure no one was around, then leaned over and peered into the tunnel. The tracks headed off into the darkness, and there was more garbage down there, what might be a colorful candy wrapper, a soda can, but mostly all was black, just different shapes and degrees of black.

"It's not the right one," Mitchell said without looking up.

"How do you know?"

He didn't answer. His eyes were locked in an unfocused stare. He was probably still high from smoking with Bruce. With that thought, Laura felt a shiver run down her spine, as if she were bracing herself, as if Bruce were right behind her. Her body reacted before her mind could assure her that Bruce was far away, back in Woodstock, doing whatever it was he did during the day.

Maybe Mitchell wasn't high from smoking. Maybe he had taken acid again.

What if we miss this train? Laura wished her father would meet them at the bus terminal.

The sound of the train got louder. Laura stepped back. She could feel the heat forcing its way ahead of the vibrations. There was always the momentary panic as the subway train pulled up. How would they know if this was the right one? Where was it heading? When would it stop next? How would they know when to get off? Laura turned back to look at her brother, realizing she relied on him completely and he had no concern for her at all. That combination didn't make for a good outcome.

"Maybe it *is* our train." The roar threatened to drown her out completely. Laura had to shout.

"So, if you think it's ours, you can get on it," Mitchell said. The train thundered, and spit and screeched, straining to stop. Car after car flew by until slowly the double doors presented themselves and hissed apart.

"But it's not our train," Mitchell said. He recrossed his legs and closed his eyes.

Definitely LSD, and it wasn't even noon yet (as if there were a proper time to drop acid).

The subway car was empty, and for some reason the doors on the opposite side of the train opened also. Laura could see through the middle, past the illuminated seats and linoleum tiles and shiny metal poles, to the platform on the other side. There was a boy sitting on a bench, just like Mitchell was, only there was something unusual about this boy.

He was holding a camera, twisting the lens and then lifting it to his face. When he lowered it back down, he was looking right at Laura.

His hair was so short that Laura thought he must be in the military, maybe just returning from Vietnam, but he looked so young. The train lingered, one second, two, and then the doors shut, the subway lurched into motion, and when the last car cleared the platform, the boy on the other side was gone.

"YOU always did like those hippie girls."

Jonas threw his sneaker at his friend Nicholas. "You're an asshole, you know that? I didn't say I liked her, I said it was weird. I'm positive she didn't get on that train. I was looking right at her."

Nick had his feet up on the desk, his whole body splayed on Jonas's bed. The room was small, and getting to it meant having to walk through Lily's larger room, the one with the fireplace. More than once, Jonas had complained to his parents about how unfair that was, but of course now it was just his mom, and complaining was out of the question.

"She probably just left while the train was passing. Don't get your panties in a bunch."

Jonas ignored the comment, mostly because it was true. He found himself thinking about the girl on the other platform, a lot, trying to figure out what had happened, how she had just vanished like that, but mostly wondering if he was going to see her again. There were eight million people living in New York City, over a million and a half in Manhattan alone. But then again, people tended to take the same subway lines, maybe around the same time of day or the same day of the week. If he really wanted to, he could go back and look for her.

"You're not even listening to me," Nick snapped. He pulled his feet off the desk, along with a few papers, a book, and an iPod.

"Hey, watch it." Jonas bent down to pick it all up.

Jonas and Nick had been best friends since

P.S. 211. They were thrown together as partners for math league in third grade, having both scored highest.

That was seven years ago. They were kneeling in the corner in Mrs. Tempe's room, working on division work sheets.

"My knee hurts," Nick said. He shifted to his bottom, cross-legged.

"Your high knee or your low knee?" Jonas asked. He knew it was a stupid joke — so second grade — but he still got a kick out of saying it. Besides, math was boring.

"My what?" Nick asked. He rubbed his left leg. "My high knee, I guess. Or maybe it's my low knee. Is this my high knee or my low knee? What?"

It took Nick several long seconds, while Jonas fell into convulsions of laughter, to get the joke, and it was the beginning — just like at the end of that old movie *Casablanca* — of a wonderful friendship.

"Sorry. Look, if you're so obsessed, why don't you go back and look for her?"

"You can't just go look for someone in the subway," Jonas said.

But he was staring out the window, trying to figure out the best way to do exactly that. Tomorrow maybe, around nine. Or ten? Ten twenty? Jonas tried to remember if he had looked at his cell right about the time he saw the girl across the tracks. Her face flashed into his mind.

"I'll tell you what," Nick said. "I'll even go with you." He jumped to his feet with a bounce or, given his size, more of a thud. "C'mon."

"Now?"

"Why not?"

"Well, it's Saturday, for one thing."

"Yeah, and—?"

"Well, if you go by the theory that the best way to find someone is to, at least, look for them at the same time you saw them last, then today and right now would not be ideal. Especially someone I don't even know lives here."

"You got something better to do today?" Nick asked.

Jonas ran his finger over the grime that always settled on the sill no matter how clean it was. What was it exactly that collected in the air of this city and stuck to flat surfaces? Exhaust from the cars in the street? Skin cells from the millions of humans? Whatever it was, it was black. And a constant.

"You know how they say there's only one thing in the universe that's constant?" Jonas started. "Change. Change is the only constant in the universe. And left alone, all things return to chaos."

Nick was at the door. He didn't seem very interested in theories of change and entropy.

"Well, that's not exactly true," Jonas went on. "There's New York City grime. That never changes, does it?"

"You coming?"

"Yeah." Jonas grabbed his jacket off the floor. "Coming."

INSIDE the subway car was more disgusting than the station, if that was even possible. The linoleum floor was sticky, and now so were the bottoms of Laura's work boots. It bothered her, the thought of some gross substance being transferred to her shoes. Marcia Brady would never have to wear shoes this ugly in the first place — though it was actually Jan, the middle sister from *The Brady Bunch,* that Laura most identified with. Jan Brady was the one no one liked, the one that always got in trouble. She was jealous and conniving.

Focusing on *The Brady Bunch* wasn't working. The subway jostled all of its passengers forward. People got on and off without thinking about it. Mitchell was dozing again in his seat.

Laura tried to concentrate on the police officer standing by the door between cars. He stood perfectly still, looking out the back window to where kids sometimes liked to ride between the cars. His gun was only partially visible, snapped into a holster with its handle jutting out, but his wooden billy club was fully exposed. Did he really hit people with that club? Like kids riding between the cars?

Would he use it on Bruce if he saw what he did? But then again, nobody ever saw what Bruce did.

The last time her mother took Laura shopping, she bought her a bra. She made Laura pick one out.

"What for?" Laura said. She was entering high school, but a couple of tight undershirts had done the trick so far.

The hypocrisy, of course, was that her mother had given up wearing a bra completely, along with her panty hose and cardigan sweaters.

"For Bruce's sake," her mother told her.

Laura felt her face burn with embarrassment and her stomach knot. She was already plenty afraid of Bruce. He had a quick temper, lots of facial hair, and a fast hand that often found its way across the back of Laura's head when he didn't like something she was doing.

No. Laura was certain that no matter how poorly she behaved or how hard her life was, Jan Brady never experienced anything like this.

"Next stop." Mitchell knocked his knee into hers as a signal and stood.

"I know," Laura said. She didn't. She took hold of the metal bar and got out of her seat. The police officer didn't even look her way. Maybe if he had, maybe if he had asked if she was all right, maybe she would have told him about Bruce, told him everything. Sometimes it's easier to talk to a stranger, the way ladies tell everything to their hairdressers.

Laura turned back, but the policeman had gotten up and was wandering farther away, down the middle of the subway car.

Laura and Mitchell made their way through the crowd to stand close to the doors and wait for the train to stop. The car was full. Two people had already taken the seats vacated by Laura and her brother. People stood body to body, but a youngish teenage boy in a floppy, wide-brimmed hat pushed ahead of Laura and stood just inside the space between her body and the doors that would open any second. Laura watched as the teenager took out what looked like a drill bit. She might have been afraid, but instead she watched as he scratched letters into the metal on the wall. Nearly every inch of the subway car was already covered with sprawling spray-painted graffiti, mostly black, nothing really legible, some red, and in this car, much of the windows was blotted out with yellow of no particular design, but the boy found a tiny space, and on it he carved his name. "Spike," he wrote, and the date: "October 8, 1972."

4

JONAS hadn't seen his father in four months. At first (after Lily accepted the fact that her dad wasn't perpetually hospitalized with chronic kidney stones), his dad would come by the apartment on Saturdays, sometimes Sundays. Mostly it was to see Lily, Jonas figured, and so everyone could pretend that he wasn't going right back to his girlfriend's after watching *Dora the Explorer* on TV or playing a rousing round of Candy Land. As if not mentioning it made it not true.

Their mom would always leave the apartment during those visits and stay out longer than she needed to in order to avoid seeing their dad. When she came back, she would walk in tentatively, as if she didn't belong, and then begin cleaning ferociously, as if reclaiming her territory. But after a while, after one or two birthday parties or a playdate took priority for Lily, or their dad had something else to do and couldn't make it on a particular weekend, the visits slowed down, and eventually they stopped. Jonas suspected that his dad was arguing to have "the kids"—by which he meant Lily—come to his new place, where he lived with Dingbat (as she was known in their house), but that his mother would never go for that.

So imagine his surprise when Jonas saw his father and his girlfriend on the platform of the Fifty-ninth Street subway station, walking right toward him. It was so sudden, so out of the blue, that Jonas forgot his mission to find the "hippie" girl. He forgot Nick was right beside him. He momentarily forgot how to breathe.

Jonas saw his father immediately, but it was Lorraine who called out to him first.

"Jonas?"

He had met Lorraine only once before, the last time his father came by to visit Lily. His mother wasn't home, and his dad and his girlfriend both came to the door. Lorraine introduced herself and then—apparently—waited out on the sidewalk, talking on her cell phone or playing on her BlackBerry the whole time. Jonas was grateful she hadn't tried to come in, and he was surprised she remembered him now.

Jonas's father still hadn't figured out what was going on. He looked around as if there was someone else named Jonas that this woman might be calling out to.

Nick whispered, "Is that her? Shit, she's hot. Sorry, man, but she is."

She was, if you liked that kind of body—round, big breasts, long legs in high heels. Never Jonas's type. Not his father's type either if you judged by the woman he had been married to for the past eighteen years. Nothing like his mother.

Nick and Jonas slowed their pace but moved forward, and eventually the four were face-to-face. Jonas's father made the first awkward move. He leaned in stiffly, hugged his son, and then turned to shake Nick's hand.

"Hello, boys," he said. "Well, Nick, you've certainly grown."

"That's generally what happens," Jonas said.

Then it was quiet.

A train roared into the station, but nobody moved. Lorraine suddenly spoke up. "So, Jonas. Are we going to be seeing you one of these days?"

It was strange—like someone had given her a

different script and she was reading for the wrong movie. *Like, hey, maybe you haven't noticed but my dad was married when he started shtupping you, and now my whole family is totally fucked up. So, when are you going to be seeing me? Probably never.*

"Seriously?" Jonas said. "We gotta go." He started walking away, and then, just like it *was* a movie, a trio warming up against a wall — violin, guitar, and bagpipes, of all things — started their woeful music.

"There's no cause to be rude," his father said.

"Well, technically you could . . ."

But his father raised his hand and cut him off before Jonas could continue. Jonas watched as his father protectively took Lorraine's arm and led her away as if from a contaminated dump site.

"What the hell was that?" Nick asked. They sat down on the same bench where Jonas had been sitting the day before when he had seen the girl who he so badly wanted to find again.

"What?"

"That. *That.* Your dad. What the hell?"

"I don't know," he said. "It just came out."

"Damn." Nick shook his head.

Jonas was silent, still struggling in his mind with the image of his dad and that woman touching. She had taken his arm? Or had he taken hers?

Nick and Jonas both looked straight ahead at the platform on the other side.

"Is that where she was sitting?"

Jonas nodded. "Yeah."

"Does she have brown hair? Long, parted in the middle?"

Jonas felt the beat of his heart quicken. "Yeah." He looked around for her.

"Is she kind of slim and really, really pretty?"

"Yeah, where?"

"Is that her, right there? Walking toward us?"

It was an old woman, the kind who might be a bag lady but then again might just be someone's grandmother who wore too many layers of clothing. And carried a lot of plastic bags.

"Oh, fuck you, Nicholas. I'm not in the mood."

"Sorry."

Jonas slouched down on the bench. "You're sorry a lot."

"I guess so, but I really am. I was just trying to take your mind off your shitty dad."

He was, wasn't he? Shitty. But it really wasn't for anyone else to say.

"Sorry," Nick said. "Again. I know, yes. I'm sorry a lot."

"It's all right," Jonas said. "So am I, I guess."

LAURA noticed her brother had slowed his pace. The sprint he had led her on as soon as they got out of the subway ended as they turned onto the avenue and neared the apartment.

The doorman recognized them and opened the door.

"You here till Sunday?" he asked. He sat back down on his stool and swiveled around toward the phone and the switchboard. He would need to call up first to let their father know they had arrived.

Mitchell actually stopped walking to answer. "Yeah."

They weren't the only kids whose parents were divorced, but Laura didn't know too many others. Maybe Mitchell was ashamed, maybe that's why he seemed deflated as they walked into the lobby, but Laura was just sad. As much as she feared being home with Bruce, as much as she fought with her mother and lived like she had been dropped onto an alien planet, the more she wanted to stay there, the more she wanted to belong. To her mother. With her mother. There was the lure of seeing her dad, of TV and hamburgers and chocolate milk, but almost as soon as she got to her dad's, she felt desperate to attach to her mother again, and Sunday seemed like a million hours away.

"Your kids are here," the doorman spoke into the black receiver. He hung up and nodded to Laura and Mitchell. "Go on up."

It would take all weekend for her to feel comfortable with her dad again, to reattach to him, to remember him and feel him as her daddy again, but then it would be just about time to go back.

Laura and Mitchell rode the elevator in silence. It was easier not to go there and start worrying about Sunday, easier to just wait out the weekend. The door to their dad's apartment was cracked open for them to come in.

"You still haven't cut your hair?"

Their dad's first words.

They were directed at Mitchell, who didn't bother to respond. Her dad wasn't the only one obsessed with hair; it was everywhere. There were lots of jokes and comments, cartoons about not being able to tell a boy from a girl anymore. There was one *Lighter Side* comic where a guy tries to pick up a shapely-looking figure with long blond hair sitting at a bar, only to find out the girl is really a guy. Laura saw that one in *Mad* magazine.

There were a few familiar things in their dad's apartment, furniture Laura remembered from their Brooklyn apartment: the narrow wooden side table that opened up for eating dinner, paintings that she used to lie on the floor and stare at. Her dad was in advertising. He was the art director for a firm on Madison Avenue, but once upon a time, he had wanted to be an artist; once upon a time, he *was* an artist, and it might have been part of the reason their parents split up. Their mother reminded him of everything he couldn't be, everything he had given up. Young, for one thing.

Laura knew that before he had gotten married, her dad had taught some studio art courses at Pratt Institute. Some of his larger Abstract Expressionist oil paintings now hung in the apartment. Everything else had gone to their mother. But not the table and not the paintings.

While her dad ran his commentary on Mitchell's long hair and blue jeans ("Only farmers wear overalls. . . . Don't you care about your appearance . . . ?"), Laura fell into the one painting she had loved as a little girl. The colors swirled around, burnt sienna, cadmium orange. She knew it wasn't supposed to *be* anything, but she rode a horse in the tiny bump of raw umber, and she smelled a Prussian blue flower that no one saw.

"Laura? Are you listening to me? Or are you smoking marijuana too?"

"What?" She whirled around. Mitchell had gone into the bathroom. Lucky he hadn't heard that. He'd be out the door.

Her dad put out his arms. "Sorry, baby. Your brother's just got me worked up. C'mon, let's get you something to eat."

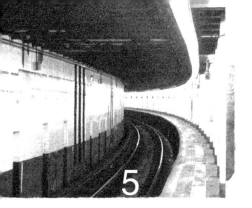

5

LAURA wasn't Jewish, not that she knew of, but she wished she were. At least that way she'd have a history of being a victim and a history of survival. She'd have a whole nation behind her. And there would be witnesses.

It wasn't that Laura envisioned her situation like that of being in the Holocaust. No, it wasn't that at all, but it was something about the way the whole world had turned its eyes away, even when the whole world knew what was going on. Or should have known. Of course they knew. So every time she felt hungry or cold, or felt the dark presence of Bruce at her back, she measured it in her mind against the annex, against Auschwitz, against Babi Yar.

She read firsthand accounts of the horrors people had survived—children, teenagers, girls, climbing out of bloody pits and living to tell about it. The key was to bear witness, to survive in order to let someone know.

Three weeks had gone by before Mitchell and Laura came back to the city to visit their dad. The subway ride had been uneventful, and her dad had even lightened up on the hair-cutting issue. He was probably playing chicken with Mitchell, but it wasn't going to work, Laura knew it.

After she read Anne Frank's diary in seventh grade, she had even lied about being Jewish at Rob Schiff's bar mitzvah, telling a group of out-of-town girls that her mother was Jewish but had converted to Christianity in order to escape from Germany during World War II.

"So, how old is your mother?" one of the girls asked.

It was too late to try to do the math.

"You don't look German."

And the whole thing started to fall apart.

"I gotta go," Laura said quickly. She rushed out of the lobby back into the catering hall, where Rob's grandfather was cutting a big loaf of bread.

Now walking down Fifth Avenue by herself, Laura could imagine herself Jewish: a survivor, albeit a survivor who'd just eaten a bologna, mustard, and potato chip sandwich; her dad even had Wonder bread and whole milk and Nesquik. She could pretend she lived in the city. She walked with a quicker pace, as if she had someplace to go and knew how to get there.

There wasn't as much psychedelic fashion in Midtown as there was downtown. Here were businessmen in suits, and women who still wore panty hose and, most likely, bras. And looking into the windows of the famous department stores on Fifth was like watching a frozen television screen. Everything was perfect and beautiful on TV.

Laura stopped in front of Saks, although she knew it made her appear to be a tourist; only visitors to the city stared into the display windows or looked up at the tall buildings, but as much as Laura wanted to belong, she couldn't help doing both.

A very skinny man wearing a tight jumpsuit was behind the glass, setting up a display. One of the mannequins was already dressed in a red-and-green-checked maxi dress. The other one was outfitted in the same material but was wearing a bell-bottom pantsuit. Everything reflected December and a Christmas that was still more than a month away. There was even fake snow on the floor of the display. The man inside the window glanced—or glared—at Laura, then ignored her and continued working. He was certainly not a visitor to New York.

He draped the maxi-dressed mannequin in love beads, and on the bell-bottom girl he placed a pointy red Santa hat. Over each, he dropped a short shearling jacket. He slipped a pair of gloves between the stiff fingers of each mannequin. He then affixed a round, colorful oversize peace-sign pin to each lapel.

Bruce, who had a bumper sticker on his VW that read I'M A PEACENIK hit Laura the first time when she wouldn't eat the seaweed he had served for dinner.

"It's food." His face was dark and unfamiliar, as if Laura had never seen him before. She suddenly couldn't place who he was.

"I don't like it," she answered.

Across the table Mitchell acted as if none of this was going on, as if he was sitting at the dining-room table alone, enjoying his plate of brown rice and seaweed, as if they had never lived a different life, as if all of this was perfectly normal.

Laura hated her brother in that moment, in that moment when Bruce smacked the back of her head, thrusting her head forward. Her teeth rattled, but nothing more. No big deal. Laura felt the blow for several more seconds, fear and anger tracking along with her red blood cells, and she calculated the amount of milk needed to wash down the salty black crap on her plate.

Where was her mother? In the kitchen? At the table?

Had anyone seen? Had everyone?

Laura knew Bruce didn't care if she ate her dinner or not, nor did he care about anything else in her life. No, this was a battle of wills, his and hers. It was a personal war she waged for the freedom of her own body; for the power over who could touch her and who could not, for what food she would or would not put inside her. Often she lost. That day she lost, but she had put up the fight. She gagged down the seaweed, and when Laura looked up, everyone was gone.

Bergdorf Goodman was across the street, as was Chanel and Tiffany's, and if she remembered correctly, FAO Schwarz was along here somewhere. Nothing in that store had ever interested her, not even when her grandmother acted as if it was a New York destination unto itself, a child's paradise. Laura never liked dolls, but she loved her Nana, and she now owned an entire collection of oddly large and gaudily overdressed Madame Alexander dolls from around the world. Laura cringed to think how her Nana would feel if she knew that half of those expensive dolls were somewhere in the woods behind her house and the rest were naked or lost entirely. Laura tried to remember how they had gotten in that state, and before she knew it, without thinking, she had walked twenty blocks north.

"THIS is your great-adventure idea?" Jonas asked. "Going to the Met?"

Yesterday had proved a bust when it came to finding the imaginary hippie girlfriend, and besides, after bumping into his father, Jonas had just felt like going back home. Now it was Sunday, and another adventure was to be found; at least, that's how Nick phrased it.

"Yeah, hottest girls in New York. You know that." They stood in front of the steps to the museum. It was one of those especially warm October mornings, the sun like a whitewash over the city. "Nothing like a babe that's bored."

"Babe?"

"Just c'mon." Nick started up the steps, two at a time.

"I see those mummies really got you turned on."

To a degree, of course, Nick was right. There were a lot of pretty girls hanging out at the Metropolitan

Museum of Art. It was fairly crowded, but then again, it always was.

Jonas let Nick buy their little metal entrance pins, a dollar for both of them.

Jonas gave him a look.

"What? It's a *suggested* fee."

"Where to?"

Nick pointed decisively across the lobby. "The Impressionist collection, of course."

Jonas didn't ask why.

The first thing Jonas always noticed in a girl was her face — if she had a pretty face and nice skin. Then her deeply colored hair, though it didn't much matter what color as long as it was healthy-looking. A slim body, not too thin, never fat. A little rounded could be nice, athletic, strong, but the skin was important. And the face.

Then, if he wasn't close enough to measure her against himself, he would quickly try to estimate her height. In middle school it was easy to be taller. Jonas towered over the other kids, girls and boys both, but lately, since eighth grade, maybe ninth, when he'd stopped growing in height, he had been more careful. Nothing was worse than being attracted to a girl only to find out she stood two or three inches taller and actually had to look down to make eye contact.

The girl across the tracks had had pretty skin and soft hair, dark and long. He couldn't get her out of his mind. He didn't bother trying, even while Nick was laying out his plan for how to pick up blasé female art students.

Jonas looked across the exhibit room. Velvet ropes hung between low brass stands surrounded each painting, creating a distinct space into which visitors could not enter. They kept people from getting too close to the Monets, the Renoirs, the Cézannes. But this dude by the far wall was standing inside, his face nearly touching the canvas. His hands were moving as if he were re-creating the brushstrokes.

"Hey, check that guy out." Jonas nudged Nick.

"Who? Where?"

The "art lover" appeared to be a teenager not much older than Nick and Jonas, if at all older. Probably Hispanic, longish hair, retro sneakers and running clothes, an odd, floppy hat.

"He's totally going to get tossed," Jonas said, turning to Nick.

"Where?" Nick said, looking around. "Where?"

Jonas lifted his chin slightly to indicate where the kid was standing, or where he had just been standing, the kid who had stepped over the ropes. A security guard was bound to show up any second, and maybe there'd be a scuffle or something exciting to liven things up, but he was gone.

"Where? Who?" Nick asked again.

"Nothing."

They hung around awhile, but there were no pretty girls, or at least no pretty girls who seemed interested in anything but the paintings. "It's better in the summer," Nick reminded them both. "More European girls on vacation."

"Let's go," Jonas said.

Nick agreed. "Falafel?"

"Sure."

HER dad hadn't started dinner, Laura was glad to see. It meant she could have some input, maybe make the whole thing herself, as long as Mitchell was busy doing something else, like watching TV. For a hippie, he sure liked *Adam-12* and *Mission: Impossible.*

On her way back downtown to the apartment, Laura had passed a couple clinging fiercely to each other. They were young, and the smell of patchouli and marijuana lingered after she had passed them. He wore a military jacket festooned with yellow fringe, and striped bell-bottoms, and she a long, velvet tie-dyed dress, but it was the way they walked, so closely connected, that stuck in her mind. It was weeks ago already, and no chance she'd ever see that boy again, from across the subway platform. He had also been wearing an army jacket. His didn't have the brass buttons or the yellow fringe, though, and come to think of it, she had no idea why she was even remembering him again.

"I'll start supper, Dad," Laura called out.

She took out three TV dinners, her favorite: Salisbury Steak. She peeled back the thick aluminum foil and stuck them in the oven. She opened a jar of Mott's Applesauce, all blended like baby food, sugar and all. Her mouth was already watering. She put out three glasses, a container of milk, and the ketchup (her dad liked ketchup on everything, a habit he claimed had resulted from his years serving in Korea).

"I met this guy named Spike today," Laura said out loud.

The apartment was small; there wasn't really anywhere you could go and not hear someone talking in the kitchen, but no one answered.

She started talking to herself: "He's Spanish. He's an artist. I met him at the museum. At the Metropolitan Museum of Art."

"Oh, yeah?"

Her dad came out of the bedroom. The door to

the guest room, where Laura and Mitchell had folding cots pushed against opposite walls, was closed. Mitchell must be in there, doing God knows what.

"Yeah, he was really cool."

Her dad took a cigarette out of his pack. He tapped it on the counter, put it to his lips, and struck a match. While he smoked, he leaned against the sink and looked out the tiny window to the window across the way.

"You know better than to talk to strangers." He drew in on the smoke and exhaled slowly. Marijuana smelled—skunky, earthy, and sweet—but tobacco just plain stank.

"That's bad for you, you know, Dad," Laura said. "It says so right on the box."

Her dad smiled. "It says it *may* be bad for you, sweetie. It hasn't killed me yet. I've been smoking since I was eleven."

"All the more reason to stop." Laura pulled open the oven to check on their dinners. The triangle side dishes of mac and cheese were just about to bubble. "Anyway, it doesn't say that. It says the surgeon general has determined that it *is* bad for your health. Look."

Her dad picked up the box from the counter and turned it over thoughtfully in his hand. "Hmm, so it does. And what does that have to do with talking to strangers? What were you doing way up there anyway?"

"Nothing. Walking."

"So you decided to go to the Met?" Her dad took another drag of his cigarette. He turned his head and blew the smoke away from Laura. His whole body relaxed. When she was little, her dad used to take her to openings, galleries, and museums all over the city. He held her hand, she held tightly to his, and she listened to his explanations for the squiggly lines and the big blotches of color on the canvases.

"I did," Laura answered.

"And this Spike was there?"

"Yeah."

He was. He had been studying the paintings like an art student, his face as close as he could get, right up to the canvas as if singling out each brushstroke, the delineation between colors, the gradation of tones.

"I know you." Laura stood beside him.

"Yeah?" The boy didn't seem surprised.

"You're Spike." She could see his name scratched into the wall of the subway car.

Now he turned to her. "How do you know that?"

"I saw you," Laura answered. "On the subway. Are you an artist?"

"I'm a writer." There was an aggressiveness to his voice. Laura instinctively took a step away.

The boy softened. "I mean we're called writers, not artists. You saw my tag?"

Laura nodded.

"Good," the boy said, and started to walk away. "You'll see more of it. I'm getting up all over. Keep an eye out."

"I will," Laura called after him.

He was kind, not dangerous. Laura had felt that. She suddenly wanted to tell her father about Bruce. Things are not all that they seem; people are not what they seem. Her dad would want to know that, wouldn't he?

Her dad stubbed his cigarette out in the sink. It hissed.

"Why don't you go and tell your brother dinner's ready. I'll take these out of the oven."

But the truth was, people just wanted to believe what was easiest, that a line from A to B was straight. There is no one behind the curtain.

"Sure, Dad," Laura answered. She knew her father didn't want to walk into the guest room and smell something he'd have to address. He looked tired; Laura was sure he didn't feel like getting into a conflict.

A to B is easier.

6

THE absolute ironic truth was that she had been the one who introduced her mother to Bruce in the first place. It was just after her parents' split, after her mom moved the three of them to Woodstock. Richard Nixon was president of the United States, and Apollo 9 launched the first lunar module. They made everyone in school crowd into the library to watch the redocking on closed-circuit TV that afternoon.

Laura's mom had rented a normal-looking, average *Brady Bunch* ranch house on a dirt road that ran off from the very top of a horseshoe street a few miles from town. The mailman didn't drive up the dirt road, so four plain mailboxes had been set up on a wooden plank at the top of the street's curve, plus one that was wildly psychedelic.

Painting that mailbox had been Philip's idea. Philip was Laura's mother's first boyfriend after the divorce. In hindsight, which is of course twenty-twenty, Laura wished she had liked Philip more. She didn't dislike him, but the whole thing was so weird, and it seemed to have happened so quickly. One year her mom was sitting, her hair curlers covered with a plastic dryer cap attached by a hose to a roaring box of hot air, watching Jack LaLanne on television, and the next she was outside in overalls and a tank top, painting yin/ yang symbols on their new mailbox while her blond long-haired boyfriend rubbed her shoulders.

For the newcomers flocking to Woodstock in 1969, it may have been another Summer of Love, but for the teachers, the parents of the other third-graders, the principal, the mailman, the town librarian, and all the other grown-ups that Laura came in contact with, it was business as usual. It was "America, Love It or Leave It." This hippie movement was an unwelcome, un-American annoyance, and if not downright dangerous, then certainly unhygienic. The town may have been invaded by musicians and *longhairs,* but the school was having none of it. Once you entered the doors of Woodstock Elementary School, you'd never know there was a zealous revolution going on outside. Laura never could have explained this to her mother.

The disparity began a game of survival.

Laura picked out Jamie Stein immediately at the Woodstock Sunday picnic, the final town picnic before school began. Her black hair was flying wild. She wore work boots, untied, no socks, and a long patchwork dress. Jamie looked like a miniature version of all the grown-ups hanging around on their Indian-print bedspreads, passing joints, except that she was running. Laura followed Jamie into the woods, along the worn paths that bordered the town green.

"Wanna go on the swings?" Jamie called out. This wild girl seemed to embody what being a hippie could or should truly be: free, loving, and willing to befriend anyone. It was just what Laura needed, moving into a new house, a new town, and a new school; she needed a guide, someone on the inside and the outside, someone who seemed to straddle both worlds.

Laura didn't really have to answer, just keep up. She could barely see the green lawn through the trees as the path wound farther away. Her experience up until now had been laid out in squares, concrete squares — Warren Street, Clinton Ave., Remsen Street. Three sides of the square got her to P.S. 8. Across one street and two more straight lines took her to her friend Denise's brownstone and so on. Anything farther than that had to be negotiated by an adult and usually required getting on a city bus or heading down into the subway and emerging somewhere totally different.

Now the ground below her sneakers was dirt, but Jamie seemed perfectly comfortable among the low bushes and high branches with sunlight filtering down from the sky, surrounding her.

This is the daughter my mother wants, Laura knew. She is the flower child, free and happy. *Nothing like me.* Maybe Laura could be more agreeable, less trouble, less square. Less Jan Brady and more Laurie Partridge. Maybe, with a friend like Jamie.

"Wait a minute." Jamie stopped suddenly.

Laura was quiet. The sounds of the town picnic were far away. If she had to, she could probably find her way back. Jamie moved off the path, a few steps into the bushes, and hiked up her skirt.

It wasn't as if Laura hadn't peed in semipublic before — once, at Jones Beach when the line to the girls' bathroom was so long. But her mother had been there, holding up a towel and shielding her. And as far as Laura could tell now, Jamie wasn't just peeing.

"I bet you'll be in my class this year," Jamie chatted away. "I hope we don't get Mrs. Crutcher. She's the meanest sixth-grade teacher."

Jamie reached out and tore some leaves from

whatever vegetation was growing beside her low crouch. "I heard that from my brother. You have an older brother, don't you?"

Laura nodded.

"I saw your brother," Jamie went on. "He's cute." She stood up, but Jamie never pulled up her underpants. Laura realized she hadn't had any on to pull down in the first place. Jamie leaped back out onto the path and started off.

"C'mon. The playground's right over here. Hopefully no one will be on the swing."

As luck would have it, a week later Laura *was* assigned to Mrs. Crutcher's sixth-grade classroom. Her mother left her school records with the main office, handed Laura her lunch box, and ruffled her hair.

"Be groovy" was her mother's advice. *Nobody really used that word, did they?*

"We have a new student this year." Mrs. Crutcher had her hands on Laura's shoulders, and it didn't feel pleasant. She would let go when she wanted Laura to sit down, when she decided *where* she wanted Laura to sit, and not a minute before. "Her name is Laura Duncan. Can everyone say hello to Laura?"

Except for the fact that everyone was white in Woodstock Elementary School, the class looked fairly familiar. Boys and girls sitting at desks; cubbies and a metal sink at the back of the room; a blackboard and erasers; and the teacher's desk at the front. Mrs. Crutcher wore a plain cotton dress and nylon socks, the kind that came to about calf height and then squeezed the fat around her leg.

Laura looked at the faces looking at her. The boys had crew cuts. The girls wore dresses and kneesocks. They probably all had mothers who sat under hair dryers at night, and fathers who went to work in the mornings. Except for Jamie Stein.

Jamie had a leather headband tied around her forehead, which she would be, later in the day, requested to remove. She was smiling widely and waving her hands.

"Well, then, Laura, I see you have a friend already." Mrs. Crutcher released her grip. "You can take the desk behind Miss Stein." Laura wasn't sure that was the best idea after all, but she sat down and smiled.

And Bruce was the boarder. He rented one of the rooms in the huge house that Jamie's mother owned. He stood in the doorway to his room the first time Laura went to visit. Laura didn't look at him very closely. She was taking in the overwhelming smell of incense, the strings of beads hanging in the doorway, the abundance of pillows, the wooden bowl filled with marijuana (*Mary Jane,* as Jamie identified it) that sat on a stand in the center of the living room. But she would always remember his presence, dark and quiet, and in her mind, Laura would torture herself with the knowledge that it was *her* friendship with Jamie that had brought her mother to this house, that had made it possible for her mother to meet Bruce, then promptly dump the blond-haired Philip. Adding to the irony, Jamie's mother sold their house a few months later and left Woodstock. They moved to New York City to open a head shop down in the village.

Bruce, with nowhere else to go, moved in with Laura and Mitchell and their mom.

Laura had brought this upon herself; if she ever did tell her father, it would all come back to that. It was her fault. And it was her destiny.

OF course he couldn't be in love. With a fantasy? A face? The most fleeting of images from across a subway track? It was pretty stupid. It was beyond stupid.

It was like there were two sides to his brain, two voices in his head, two realities existing at the very same time. One created elaborate dreams and romantic stories about this girl whose name he didn't know but who had nice hair and skin, and the other shot it all down.

Jonas was scrambling eggs, three eggs in a bowl.

His toast had already popped up and was getting cold. He pushed the toaster button down again. He could never seem to get the timing right when he made breakfast or lunch. It was nearly one on Sunday—afternoon already. He had his dog-walking job to get to. He was late already, but the dogs never told on him. Today he had only one, a Labradoodle right down the hall.

Jonas's mind wandered to her face. He had seen it for only a few moments, but he could recall every detail. The girl was sitting there on the bench. She had a retro look, not a phony-retro look but a real one. She had a hat on, a knitted cap, and she played with a strand of her hair that hung loose around her shoulder. She twisted it between her thumb and ring finger, which for some reason Jonas had noticed.

Oh, my God. Even more stupid. How could he possibly have seen that far? It was impossible. And for Christ's sake, who cares? The butter in the frying pan was smoking.

"Oh, shit," Jonas said out loud.

Love sucks anyway. Look at his own parents.

Jonas swirled the pan around and dumped in the eggs. They sizzled and began to cook immediately. Love sucks, but Jonas hadn't "bumped" into the girl again in weeks, so none of this mattered. His toast popped up, charcoal black.

JONAS had seen the e-mail on his father's computer, and so he had read it. It wasn't like his dad was a technological idiot or anything. If he left it open, even with the underwater blowfish wallpaper scrolling and bubbling across the screen, he must have known someone could read it. Never mind Jesus, what would Freud say?

There are no accidents, that's what he would say.

"Hard Love" was the subject heading, and it was addressed to SongCatcher@gmail.com. The e-mail opened with *My dearest heart.* Jonas knew immediately it wasn't for his mother. Besides, his mother's e-mail was Mom32, the address she made up when AOL was still pretty new, at least to her, and she didn't realize it would become her "name." She never bothered to change it. Certainly not to Mom46.

Jonas read the e-mail as if he were reading a book, a novel, someone else's words, a fictional life that told of yearning and loss. It didn't sound anything like his dad, unless his dad was actually a poet and not an investment banker at HSBC. As a young man, Jonas's dad had wanted to be an actor, but *his* father, Jonas's grandfather, had made him give up summer stock to get a real job just as he was getting some attention, or so went the story. Maybe this was his father's way of feeling alive, getting back at *his* father.

> My one and only love. My body comes alive when
> it is with your body. My heart beats only in rhythm
> with yours. My eyes see only the world in which
> you exist. There is no world for me without you.
> I promise, we will someday be together forever.
> It was meant to be, and with our strength we will
> make it happen. Last night—

Jonas stopped reading. His hand reflexively covered his mouth and he ran for the bathroom. The nausea lessened as he leaned his hands on the sink and tried to breathe. Everything here was normal: a pimple of white toothpaste stuck on the faucet; the brushes that didn't quite fit in the toothbrush holder but leaned precariously to the left and right; his mother's hair in the drain; the smell of his father's aftershave; his sister's plastic Elmo baby cup she refused to give up.

He peered up into the mirror. Jonas looked like his dad. Everyone said that so often, he figured it to be true. Even as a baby he'd had his father's features; whereas most babies have little pug noses, Jonas had a long, thin nose. And he had his father's eyes, heavy on the upper lid, round, light brown. Lily looked like their mother. They paired off that way, father/son, mother/daughter.

Who was his father writing to? Who was *My dearest heart? My one and only love?* What the fuck was this? What did this say about all of them — about his mother, about their family? What did this say about everything that had come before?

The feeling that he was going to throw up came springing back. His mouth filled with saliva in preparation; his stomach muscles tightened. Jonas lowered himself to his knees and lifted the toilet seat.

At least, he assumed it was a woman. Last year, in ninth grade, the father of one of the kids in his class turned out to be gay. Married twenty-three years, three kids, and now he lived in an apartment in the East Village with Pierre.

So, see? Things could be worse. Jonas let the scrambled eggs slide onto his plate, buttered his toast, and poured a second cup of coffee. Right now, it was a relatively peaceful Love-Sucks Sunday afternoon.

7

WHEN he had almost completely stopped thinking about that girl, Jonas saw her again. He had just gotten on the 6 train, and this time she was sitting inside the subway car, all the way at the other end, leaning her head against the wall, reading a book. He was sure it was her. It had been nearly two months. Jonas's first instinct was to pull out his phone and text Nick.

No bars.

But it was definitely her.

The subway car was half full. Two people, an older woman and a younger man, were arguing loudly in the center of the train, but while most of the riders had glanced up to make sure there was no immediate threat to their own well-being, engrossed in her book, the girl kept her eyes down. She was even prettier than Jonas remembered. Her hair was down and tucked behind her ears — shiny, curly, like a wave that is stilled in time. She was wearing jeans with a fabric patch on one knee. It looked genuinely homemade. Jonas was a sucker for a girl in jeans.

Two more people got on and sat down. It was a warm December, but it still seemed odd that nobody was wearing winter clothing. But then the subway car was warm, with air blowing in from the vents above. Jonas took off his gloves and sat down. It was one of those old cars that should have been taken out of service long ago, its seats dirty and scribbled on and cracked. Jonas's father was always complaining about the MTA, higher fares and fewer trains. The people in their seats rocked slightly as the train jerked into motion, but Jonas kept his eyes on the girl, waiting for the moment when she might look up from her book.

When the subway stopped and she did not get off, Jonas moved to the next metal pole. As the train sped into motion again, Jonas moved closer and sat down in the last open seat nearest the end of the car. He reached into his pocket and pulled out his cell phone again. It gave him something to fiddle with, an excuse for occasionally looking up reflectively, as if he were working on something. What he really wanted was to take out his camera, but he'd already decided that would look too creepy. Instead, Jonas scrolled through his address book, actually concentrating on the numbers he no longer needed or wanted.

Carmenfromdeli

DeborahB

Frank

Jonas looked up. She was still reading, playing with her hair, just like he remembered. So far she hadn't noticed him. Jonas returned to his address book.

Pizzaon3rd

Robert

KevinFixler

Now, there was a name he could get rid of. What an asshole he turned out to be. He and Jonas had been pretty tight until ninth grade, when Kevin went to their English teacher and asked to be regraded on a joint-writing project they had done. Kevin felt his half of the work deserved better than a B+.

Screw him.

Delete.

The girl closed her book, a hardcover. Jonas could read the title: *The Bell Jar*. He thought he had heard of that. She looked up. He was certain she looked right at him.

Do something, or you'll never see her again.

Do something.

The subway was slowing down. It got louder when it was near stopping, hissing and screeching, metal on metal. People were standing and jockeying for position toward the doors. They were eager for air, to get where they were going, or to run away from where they had been.

She looked like she was going to stand up.

Do something. Say something.

"Hi," Jonas said. He said it out loud, but did he say it loudly enough? Loudly enough to be heard over his pounding heart? He could hardly hear himself. Or just loudly enough that the old man with the grocery bags next to him would answer instead?

"Hi," she said back. "I've seen you before, right?"

"I think so," Jonas answered. The train jolted to a stop, the doors flew open, and the energy of a *whoosh* of people emptied from the train. It was Fifty-ninth Street. Lexington Ave.

"I get off here," the girl said.

"I'm Jonas." But he didn't move. He watched her body step off the train. She wore a white blouse with tiny embroidery around the neck, around *her* neck. Why couldn't he move?

"Jonas Goldman on Facebook." Finally he stood up. Finally he was able to move, but only slowly.

"What?"

"Are you on Facebook?"

"Face book?"

"Yeah." Why didn't she seem to be able to hear him?

"OK, Jonas Goldman. Well, maybe I'll see you again," she said, but she was already outside; he was still inside.

"When?"

"I come back in two weeks."

And the doors between them slid shut.

NICK had only one question: "Why didn't you just get off at her stop?"

"I don't know," Jonas said. "I just didn't think. I wasn't expecting to ever see her again. My brain just froze, I guess."

"God, you're an idiot." Nick gripped his controller and leaned his whole body to the right as if he could affect the animation on the screen, or as if it were affecting him somatically, which was more likely. "Throw your grenade."

"I know. You don't have to tell me. Oh, shit, I got sniped." There was a part of Jonas that really hated to play Call of Duty. It was violent and competitive, and everyone else who played was practically a professional assassin. He was always getting killed.

"I hate this map," Nick said. They both kept dying.

Jonas shut off the Xbox and switched back to TV.

"So, what do you think she means, 'I come back in two weeks'?" Nick asked.

"No idea."

SportsCenter was on its third rerun of the afternoon.

"Back in the city, maybe?" Jonas said. "Maybe she doesn't live here. She just visits."

"Or commutes." Nick flipped through the channels. "You have Roku? Netflix? I forget."

"Neither," Jonas told him. "And don't order another pay-per-view. My mother will kill me. What do you mean 'commutes'? She's a kid. I mean, she's like us. She doesn't work."

"She could work. Maybe she's a model." Nick put his feet up on the coffee table. "Yeah, maybe she's a fashion model. What's on your DVR? You know, Jonas, you're the only friend I have that doesn't have a TV in their own room."

Jonas bent down to pick his coat up off the floor. "I'm going out," he said.

"Where?"

"Just out. I want to shoot some film. Look." Jonas pointed to the large south-facing window. In another hour the sky would be dark, but at that moment it was yellow: winter yellow. "The light is amazing. I'll be back soon."

Nick sat up. "But this is your house," he said.

MITCHELL stopped going to visit their dad. He just stopped. Last month he was nowhere to be found when it was time to leave for Kingston to catch the bus into the city. This week, Mitchell stated he didn't want to go, and no one bothered to question him.

"But I can't find Dad's apartment by myself. Find the right subway," Laura said. She stood in the kitchen.

Her mother was washing dishes. "Sure you can." She shut the water off. "Hurry and get your stuff."

"Now?" Laura froze.

Her mother turned to face her, her hands still wet. "Laura, where is your head? It's Friday. It's your weekend to see your dad. Now, get your stuff or leave without it."

It was Friday? It was hard to keep the days straight. Sometimes it was hard to keep anything straight—names, days, homework, especially directions. Living with Bruce had forced upon her a sense of being on high alert that made it hard to focus on the present. Laura got lost a lot or, at best, temporarily turned around everywhere, walking to school, walking in school, and she certainly would walking in New York City by herself. And then there was the experience she was feeling now, panic. She didn't want to go.

She wanted to stay where she was. A body in motion stays in motion, and, well, a body at rest needs to stay at rest. Though there was nothing restful about being home, being anywhere near Bruce, Laura felt somehow more anxious about leaving, in particular alone.

"You'll be fine." But her mom looked distracted. She looked tired. She looked old, older than thirty anyway, probably because she was. Way over thirty.

Don't trust anyone over thirty.

Isn't that what they said? It was another hippie slogan that meant nothing.

But Bruce wasn't thirty yet, which made him the real thing and all the more dangerous. Apparently he had dropped out of college to live in New Mexico with the Hopi Indians and take peyote, and, according to him, he then traveled around California with Timothy Leary for a while, experimenting with mind-

expanding drugs. Somehow he ended up in Woodstock. He ended up with Laura's mother, in this house.
He wasn't even twenty-five years old.

He walked into the kitchen and into the conversation. "You'll be fine, Laura. You're almost a woman
now, aren't you?"

Bruce was wearing a Mexican wool poncho over
a pair of cutoff shorts and nothing else, Laura was
pretty sure. His beard was growing outward from
his face, making his face seem larger, and he hadn't
bathed in what smelled like quite a long time. He was
barefoot. It was April, that time of year when it was
colder inside the house than out, but Bruce seemed
immune.

"I'm only fourteen," Laura said.

"Juliet was fourteen," Bruce said.

Laura's mother glanced up from the dishes. She
looked like she was going to say something else. "Go
get your stuff, Laura."

The subway would be a piece of cake.

But, of course, it wasn't a piece of cake at all. Laura
had followed the signs to the uptown 4/5/6 lines and
stood on the platform, but she had no idea if it was
the right platform, or which train zooming by would
be the one to take her to the right stop. It was dark in

the tunnel, and she was afraid to stand too close to the edge to see farther down. A train lurched and hissed and screeched to a stop in front of her.

But Laura saw the huge spray-painted letters first: *SPIKE*. The rest of the graffiti on the car was black — thin letters, scrawled epithets, and nasty words — but this writing seemed to pop from the side of the car and demand attention. The vibrant colors, the subtle tones, the depth behind the letters, the edgy version of the Pink Panther leaning on the letter *S* and casually smoking a cigarette.

It was so common, all kinds of mess covering a train, but this mess was different. It was a beautiful mess. *S-P-I-K-E.*

I'm getting up all over. Keep an eye out.

Laura smiled.

She didn't have time to ask anyone, *Is this the 6 train?* The crowd of bodies shifted on, and Laura shifted along with it. Somehow she knew. This was the right car.

THERE were absolutely amazing photographs everywhere, on everyone's Facebook page and everyone's iPhone and Instagram, just floating around in cyberspace for eternity. People took hundreds and thousands of digital pictures; one or two, even twenty or a hundred, were bound to be great. All anyone had to do was click through them all and post the ones they liked, deleting the rest. But using film meant you never knew what was going to be a good picture, let alone a great one, until you were standing there looking at a contact sheet with a magnifying glass and deciding which to print.

Maybe nobody cared anymore, but then again, writers probably felt the same way when word processors were invented. Anyone with a story and a keyboard could write their memoir now, write the great American novel, or tweet a 140-character trope that gets retweeted and is read by hundreds of people every hour of every day.

The sun was just glancing over the tops of the highest buildings and disappearing from the street. Jonas was glad he had thought to put 400 film in his camera. He would need to shoot with his lens wide open. He had thirty-six exposures and film was cheap. What was costly was not the shot but coming back without good pictures to choose from. The light was perfect, orange gray, casting long shadows. The city seemed to reveal more the darker it got.

When he left the house, it hadn't been on his

mind — seeing her maybe — but then again, you never know. He tried not to think about it, to wait for her. It was so out of his control, and he had given her his name. If she'd wanted to, she would have found him. If she had been even remotely interested, she would have Facebooked him. He must have checked a thousand times.

No new friend requests.

Jonas held his camera in his hand and descended the stairs to the downtown subway. He had put her out of his mind as best he could, which meant he scanned the station only every other minute or two.

Jonas could hear a train pulling into the station when he swiped his MetroCard. He pushed through the turnstile. Up ahead he could see the cars slowing, colors blurring. It was a weird mess of pictures and writing. This was the second time in only a couple of weeks, not even a month, that the subway had looked like this. In fact, the last time he saw a subway car so covered in graffiti was when he saw *her*. Jonas quickened his steps; he ran toward the platform.

It was huge. It covered one whole car. Jonas thought he recognized the sly-looking feline cartoon character. The Pink Panther? And there were big bubble letters that seemed to be coming right out of the side of the train. It might have been some kind of city art project, but it really didn't look like that. It looked too real to be a reproduction. Too gritty. His heart was pounding.

Jonas immediately pulled out his camera and dropped to one knee. He wanted the whole view, tilted slightly upward; he wanted to capture the entire car. He checked the light. He adjusted the aperture and set the shutter speed. He was just about to take a series, hopefully click off three or four or six shots. The doors opened, and there she was. Jonas didn't pause and didn't think. He slipped onto the train.

8

WHEN Laura was eleven years old, her mother decided to make her a dress. It felt so perfect, like something Mrs. Brady would do, until after they had chosen the Simplicity pattern.

"How about this one?" her mother said.

The packages were stored in bins, arranged by numbered styles: skirts, pants, jackets, dresses; long, short, midi, maxi. The paper covers depicted a sketchy drawing of a model wearing a few variations of the pattern. The size and measurements were printed in the upper left-hand corner.

Laura looked up from where she had been flipping through the A-line skirts. Each drawing and each model looked more beautiful and happy than the one before. Each one made Laura's heart beat excitedly as she anticipated the life she could have when she was wearing this new dress, a Marcia Brady life. And if she couldn't be Marcia or even Jan Brady, maybe she could be Laurie Partridge; they practically shared a name, after all.

Laura's mother held up a package with an illustration of two girls on the cover, each in a variation of a tunic-style dress, one long and one short. Both girls were smiling, and the short dress was pretty enough, with the belt tied in the back and the sleeves belled out at the wrist. Laura looked down at the pattern in her hand. She slipped hers back into the bin.

"I like it," Laura told her mother. It would be nice enough, as long as it wasn't the long version, and as long as she could still pick out the material, but somehow when they got home, everything went wrong.

Laura's mother decided the dress would look cool (or had she said *groovy,* again?) if the material was turned inside out. Now the colors were muted and odd, like dripping, dull paint. Nothing like the pretty flower pattern Laura had selected in the store. Her mother decided to add lace, yellowed and torn, from an antique couch to the sleeves and the hem of the dress. And she decided on the long version, the Janis Joplin–Marianne Faithfull look.

Laura stood on the table while her mother, holding the pins in her mouth, tacked up the hem. Laura felt exposed, naked, even though she was draped in excessive, albeit drab, material, with a collar that gripped her neck, and sleeves that hung like enormous wilted flower petals trimmed with rotting lace. It was night, dark outside and not much lighter inside, so her image was mirrored in the window. In the glass she could see Bruce crouched by the woodstove, starting the fire. From time to time he looked over to where Laura stood on display. Mitchell was next to him, handing Bruce kindling, twigs and small pieces of wood, both of them most certainly high.

In the reflection everything was far away and distant. It looked like an entirely different scene — homesteaders, like *Little House on the Prairie,* the whole family safe inside their cabin, sewing, making a fire. But nothing here was safe. She didn't want this dress; she didn't want this life. She missed her dad and she missed her parents.

The next day, Laura got called into the principal's office for wearing inappropriate attire to school, and Mr. Mahoney appeared genuinely surprised by her flood of tears.

"School is not a costume party, young lady," he

told her as if she were not aware of this fact. "This is not one of those hippie communes."

It seemed to Laura to be the most absurd of ironies and not worth explaining. All she could do was cry.

It was that first year with Bruce when Laura realized there were two worlds: the world within and the world without. She could exist within, she could endure, she could dream, and she could fly. The world without, where everyone else existed, including her dad, Mr. Mahoney, even Jan Brady to a certain degree, was out of her reach.

By the time she got to high school, Laura had perfected her world within. Like in the books she was reading, the way the Jewish people survived the concentration camps, the roll calls, the hiding. Dive inside your head where you are safe. Separate yourself from the pain. Inside your head you can be in control and you can bear any pain if you know it isn't going to last. The key was figuring out when it was going to end.

SHE was even prettier than he remembered, different from any girl he had known or, to be honest, ever seen. Jonas didn't really like any of the girls at his school, who were, for the most part, entitled and high-maintenance with a ridiculously inflated sense of self-worth. But it wasn't like he was one of those guys who liked "damaged" girls. Nick had once said there was nothing better than a girl with low self-esteem. No, it wasn't like that.

Of course, he could be wrong. He had barely talked to this girl. For all he knew, it was the same-old same-old: *She's just not that into you.*

"Um, hi," Jonas said. Here she was. There was no time to consider saying anything else. The train lurched forward, and Jonas had to take a jerking step, grabbing on to the metal pole above her head in order to stop himself from falling, like a newbie, like a tourist. Only tourists stumble on the subway. This wasn't going well.

She looked at him. "Hi."

So it wasn't anything she said, obviously, but it was the way she said it. The way she smiled that let him know: It's all OK, even if you fall on your face. It's cool.

"Can I sit . . . down?" Jonas asked her.

The car was mostly empty. There was an older African-American businessman sitting at the opposite end, reading a book, and a young girl, Asian, too thin, with her hair pulled tightly back into a bun, reading nothing, looking hungry. A mother holding the handle of a stroller stood waiting for the doors to open at the next stop.

"I saw you before," Jonas said. He'd thought about saying *met*—*I met you before*—but if she didn't remember him, that would seem really weird. The train was slowing. *What if she is getting off here?* He would follow her, he decided. This time, he would get off with her, but she didn't seem to be shifting in that direction.

"I remember. Jonas."

She remembered his name. Her gaze moved to the floor just briefly, then she met his eyes again, like she was forcing herself to be confident.

"Jonas Goldman, Faceman, right?" she said. "I'm Laura."

She had a quiet voice but strong. He could smell her breath slightly: sweet and warm, like honeyed milk. She was just the right balance of shy yet poised.

Faceman?

Maybe that meant something? She was an anti-technology type. Or she was teasing him. *But teasing is a good sign, isn't it?*

The subway stopped and the woman with her toddler got off. Train rides don't last forever. Everybody gets off sometime. He felt time squeezing in on him.

"Do you live in the city?" Jonas asked. It sounded stupid. It sounded forward. *Too forward?* Everybody was wary—of strangers, of perverts, of thieves. There had been a rash of people stealing iPhones right out of people's hands on the subway.

Laura—Laura, right?—didn't have a cell phone visible. She probably hid it. Or she was one of those Neo-Luddites he had heard about, in which case she would hate him. But more likely she *was* just wary. He had been too forward. She'd never talk to him now.

"No," she answered. "I live upstate. I'm just visiting my dad. My parents are divorced. Oh, God, did I just say that?"

So she wasn't wary. She wasn't from New York, that's why.

Jonas laughed. "Mine are, too. No worries. I'm—"

Still, if he got off when *she* got off, if he, oh, just coincidentally, was going where *she* was going, then she might start to worry. But he needed to do something quickly, and the Facebook thing hadn't worked last time.

"Can I text you? You want my cell number?"

She crinkled her brow. Her eyes were brown and her lashes short but dark, and there were so many of them.

"Your what?"

"My number? So you could call me. Or I could call you?"

"Oh." Laura smiled. "Sure. At my dad's?"

That caught Jonas off-guard for a minute, like maybe she was one of those religious girls and she needed her father's permission, or she was just screwing around with him. Yanking his chain, pretending to be interested. Pretending to be nice. Several scenarios ran through his head, but you can't pretend to be so pretty, so he said, "Yeah, your dad's house is good."

She stood up. "Is this the Fifty-ninth Street stop?" She was nervous.

It made him feel good to answer. "Yeah, Fifty-ninth. And Lexington. Between Park and Third." *Good God, stop talking.*

For a second Jonas racked his brain for a reason he could be getting off here, too. He put his hand on his camera bag. He hoped she didn't think it was a man purse or anything.

"This is a camera," he said.

"I know," Laura said. She started out the open doors. "So you want my dad's phone number?" And she gave it to him, area code and all. Just like that. He had her name. And her phone number, albeit her *dad's* phone number.

She got off the train, and as fast as he could, he pulled out his phone and keyed it in.

New contact:

Laura.

HE tried every configuration. He must have typed it in wrong. Reversed a number or something. It had to be.

"I think she was just dicking you around," Nick said.

"No way."

They were at Nick's house because there was a chance (or a hope) you needed a landline to call another landline, and Jonas's mom — to save money — didn't have one.

"OK, then, maybe it's a 718 number," Nick tried.

"I tried that," Jonas said. They sat in the kitchen where the oldest phone in the United States was attached to the wall. It was olive green, all but the warped and tangled cord that had somehow turned greenish brown over the years.

Jonas's mom had been exclusively cell phones and Internet for quite a while now, even though she was completely tech-challenged. She had to call Jonas every time she wanted to record a show on the DVR. She asked Jonas to set up her cell phone. She hardly used the computer at all, and if she wasn't phobic to it before, she was now.

Jonas couldn't have explained, even to himself, why he had begun printing out his father's e-mails. He hadn't printed the first one he discovered open on his dad's desktop, but after that, Jonas had to hack into his father's AOL account and search for them. Was that why he started printing them? The sheer effort?

It took only one guess to find the password: KELLY, his father's first and only family dog. Jonas, of course, had never known Kelly, but he had heard the stories. They all had. His father talked about Kelly often, whenever they watched a dog movie, or whenever they met someone on the street with a similar-looking dog. There was even a picture on the refrigerator of Jonas's dad as a little boy with his arm around his beloved beagle mix — or rather, there used to be.

And now that he had the password, all of his father's e-mails — new, old, sent, and saved — were there for the viewing. And he had her name: Lorraine, otherwise known as SongCatcher@gmail.com. Each time he logged on, it was like a game Jonas was playing with himself not to get caught. It gave him an odd, thrilling beating of his heart. It reminded Jonas of playing hide-and-seek when he was little during summer vacations on Long Island. Someone would hide their eyes and count backward, while everyone else went running, terrified, looking for a place to hide, listening to their time running out.

Ten . . . nine . . . eight . . .

Knowing he had willingly put himself in a

position to be hunted down and caught, but hoping he wouldn't be, Jonas would hide under a bush, or inside the shed of their summer rental, his heart pounding with fear and excitement.

He was careful to clear his search history so his father wouldn't see that someone had been in his e-mail. At first Jonas read only e-mails that his father had read, but the more he read, the more daring he got. He began reading e-mails his father hadn't yet read, carefully highlighting "mark as unread" when he was finished and leaving everything as it was. His father would come home from work, kiss his mother, say hello to Jonas and Lily.

"I'm just going to check my e-mails before dinner," he said.

Jonas watched as his dad put down his briefcase. He watched his calm, steady gait, like nothing was up, as if nothing were different, as he made his way into his bedroom, where he kept his laptop. Jonas kept his eyes down on his math book, or his novel, or his history notes, but his thoughts were focused on his father, on the e-mail Jonas had read earlier that day, on knowing something his father didn't yet know. Knowing that he could have deleted the e-mail, that he could affect this secret relationship. He could even write back and tell Lorraine it was all over, then delete the sent mail.

But he never did.

What he *did* do, however, was print out the e-mails and hide them in his room, at the very back of his desk drawer, instead.

"Let me try," Nick said. "What's the number again?"

Jonas had it memorized by now, but Nick still had no luck. When they called the number Jonas had in his cell phone, they got some old lady who told them if they called again she would report them to the police. Other configurations yielded fax machine buzzes or other wrong numbers.

"You must have heard wrong, then," Nick tried.

"Yeah, maybe. Or she's dicking me around." But somehow Jonas didn't really believe that.

LAURA couldn't stop thinking about him, Jonas, the boy from the subway, and she was glad her brother hadn't come to New York with her. She found herself staying inside, listening for the phone to ring.

"We have to go out to eat," her dad said. "Besides, you've been in all weekend."

"I can make us eggs," Laura said.

She and her dad ate in front of the television, which was another plus in coming to her dad's, but the truth was, she didn't know whether he had eggs in the fridge or not. She could eat cereal. Her dad bought the good kinds, Froot Loops and Sugar Frosted Flakes. In fact, it would be a dream to eat cereal for dinner and watch TV. That way if the phone rang, she'd be right here to answer it. Only it didn't, other than a call from her father's accountant and one wrong number.

This Saturday night, Laura's father watched *All in the Family* (Laura agreed to watch too if her dad promised to watch *Bridget Loves Bernie* afterward), and they had scrambled eggs with cheese, toast, and bacon. The same familiar sadness came over Laura afterward as she watched her dad doing the dishes. She missed him. He was standing right in front of her, and she missed him so terribly.

When she was a little girl, if they went out someplace, she used to pretend to fall asleep in the backseat of their station wagon on the ride home. Mitchell got to sit up front, right in between their parents, looking out onto the road unfolding in front of them. There was a clear order: daddies drive, mommies sit next to them, oldest kid in front. If Daddy was at work and Mommy was driving, two kids could sit in front. It was a simple age rotation. So as long as Mitchell was alive and living at home, Laura was relegated to the backseat, but if she timed it right, she could look out the side window most of the ride, then settle down, stretch out across the seat, and close her eyes. By the time they got home, everyone thought she was fast asleep, and instead of waking her, her mom would instruct her dad to carry her up to bed.

"Careful, Hank," her mother would say. "Don't wake her up."

And Laura would feel her daddy's strong arms lifting her right out of the car and cradling her, just like when she was a baby. And even if she couldn't actually remember what it felt like to be a baby, this felt good, so good. So safe, and weightless. Her daddy was the protector of the whole world.

But now he looked so helpless and alone, laughing at Archie Bunker picking on his son-in-law. Laura could feel her heart breaking in two—two parts—one for her and one for him. He couldn't protect her anymore. She was leaving in less than twelve hours. Sunday morning she'd be back on the bus to Kingston, and her mom would be waiting for her, maybe her mom and Bruce.

After her father went to bed, Laura snuck out into the living room and called the operator.

She cupped her hand over her mouth and the receiver. "I just wanted to check if this phone is working properly," Laura whispered.

"Why, yes it is, miss. Are you having trouble with your line?"

"No, I mean, I just wanted to make sure it was working."

"It seems to be," the voice said. "Are you all right, sweetheart?"

"Yeah, I am."

The city noises, sirens and horns, were comforting. Lights moved across the ceiling as cars went by in the street.

"How old are you?"

"Fourteen," Laura answered.

"Are you home alone?"

"No, my dad's sleeping." Then Laura had an impulse to tell this nice woman everything. *I met this boy on the subway and I have no idea who he is but I gave him my number and he hasn't called. I know that sounds stupid but I think he really wants to call me. I don't know why he hasn't. Now I'm leaving and I'm going back to my mom's house where we live with her asshole boyfriend who sometimes hits me and while I'm mentioning it, my brother's an asshole, too.*

But I really like this boy. He said his name is Jonas.

But of course she didn't say any of that.

"Are you sure you're all right, then? Your phone seems to be working just like it's supposed to."

"Yeah, thanks." Laura hung up.

9

SPIKE has a real name, of course. It's Max Lowenbein, but he sure wouldn't tell anyone that. When he first started doing throw-ups, at ten, he used the tag Slug138. Then he was SuperKool for a while, but that was two years ago. It took him all winter to rack up enough spray paint for his piece, his masterpiece, a burner that would set the city on fire. Every writer, everyone who was anyone, would be talking about it, a full end-to-end train.

He had been planning it for months, benching for hours to memorize the schedules, the routes, every train, every layup, even frequenting art museums and galleries, sketching it all in his notebook. No one had done a whole train before, at least not with style. Spike had been working to perfect his style, and replacing the spray-paint cap with the fatter nozzle from Niagara Spray Starch gave him just what he needed, wider surface coverage and less drippage. He knew in his heart that he was nearly ready. The secret to life is good timing. Timing is everything.

Can't wait too long. Can't move too soon.

He had done the Pink Panther car. That was a hit. Some other writers, some dope writers like Snake131 and Lil Hawk, were still talking about it. But not his masterpiece; no, his masterpiece was still to come.

It had to be just right. It would take all night and he would need a crew. The secret to life is good timing, and good timing might require warmer weather.

IT was a month and a half before Laura returned to New York City again, to a rainy, cold January. There had been flurries when she left Kingston. Here it was freezing rain. Only a few people stood on the platform. Laura read the wall behind her while she waited. It was covered with graffiti, messages left in response to other messages, different handwriting, who knew how far apart in time.

Beatniks are worthless.

(and underneath)

Your attitude is worthless.

(underneath)

Beatniks have been extinct since 1960. Where have you been?

(underneath)

Beat the draft.

To beat is cool.

To beat-cool is not to be beat.

To beat-cool and not to be beat is nowhere.

Laura wondered if it made sense to anyone. She only vaguely knew what Beatniks were, precursors to the hippies, the Beat Generation, underground and nonconformist. Laura wondered how long ago these messages had been written, if the people who wrote them ever came back to see the responses.

She hadn't stopped thinking about him, about Jonas, but she'd tried. She'd imagined so many stories, about how the boy had called her father's apartment while she was away. She didn't talk to her dad between visits, but in her fantasy he called their house in Woodstock, about some issue or another, and then casually mentioned that some boy had called looking for her.

Jacob, Jeremy?

Jonas?

91

Yeah, that was it. He called and explained he had wanted to call over the weekend but had gotten run over by a taxi. . . . No, that was no good. . . . No matter what story she came up with, nothing really worked. If a boy wants to call you, he calls. So when Laura looked up and saw Jonas Goldman walking into the subway car, she was over him. Done. Finished. She lowered her eyes and hoped he hadn't noticed that she had seen him.

"Laura?"

He said it again before she raised her head slightly.

"I tried calling you and calling you. I think you gave me the wrong number." He sat down right beside her. He was wearing an odd jacket, some strange kind of woolly material she had never seen before. He had no umbrella, but he was the only person on the train who wasn't wet at all. *Wrong number.* Laura shifted away slightly. Her intuition was right; he was bad news, but then again, he looked so sweet, earnest, without guile.

"I must have called a million times."

And he didn't seem to mind looking eager. Most boys wouldn't have admitted that. Unless he was lying, that is.

"No, I didn't give you the wrong number. I gave you my dad's. You never called."

Laura realized that, to a degree, she had just given herself away — let him know that she had noticed he hadn't called; she had been waiting, and she probably let him hear her disappointment.

"I even checked my phone line," Laura said. "About a hundred times." She laughed. Somehow with this boy it didn't matter.

"Well, don't you have a cell phone?"

"What's that?"

Jonas made a face that Laura couldn't interpret.

"I guess you don't," he said. "Maybe I could just sit and talk to you? Wanna go to a Starbucks or something?"

She didn't want to do it again, look stupid, let on that she had no idea what he was talking about.

Her mouth opened but nothing came out.

"Coffee?" he asked.

So she answered, "Sure."

IT was just too crazy. It wasn't like everyone had poured out of the subway car and they'd simply lost track of each other in the throng. It was weirder than that. Jonas just disappeared. The doors opened. Jonas actually held out his arm to let Laura go first. She stepped onto the platform, sensing he was right behind her, and then sensing he wasn't.

She moved forward, away from the gap, out of

the way of the crowd waiting to board, and he was gone. She turned around and no one was there.

"I told you, I just got off at the wrong stop," Laura told her mother Sunday night. Her mother was reading the paper under a single floor lamp. Laura was lying on the floor sharing the light, trying to read a book.

As it turned out, her mom was at work when the phone call from New York came, and it was Bruce who spoke with Laura's dad, and it was Bruce who had to walk into town to deliver the news to Laura's mom. By the time they got back to the house and called her dad, Laura had been found.

Bruce was working in the next room, at the dining-room table, where he had a large industrial sewing machine set up. He and Mitchell were planning on building a tepee as soon as the weather got a little warmer, somewhere up in the woods behind their house. Bruce had brought in heavy white canvas and special thick thread. For some reason, anything American Indian was groovy cool.

"No, next time Mitchell will go with you. That was ridiculous. Your father was furious."

"No," Laura blurted out.

She didn't want her brother to go. If Laura was ever to find Jonas again, she had to be alone. If she was ever going to figure out what had happened when they stepped off that train, Mitchell couldn't be there. She knew that.

Bruce looked up from his work. "I'm not going to walk all the way into town again because you don't know which subway to take." He put down his stitching.

"I mean, I just made a mistake. I was fine." Laura felt something rising up her spine, like an involuntary surge of electricity. Her muscles tightened.

Mitchell would ruin everything. "I don't want Mitchell to go."

Bruce stood up.

Laura understood, as she had for a while, that it wasn't pain she was afraid of. She had experienced much worse, a fall from her bike onto gravel, a nail that went right through the bottom of her Keds, that sliver of wood that wedged directly underneath her fingernail when she ran her hand down the railing.

No, it wasn't pain. It was the anticipation.

It was fear, and it was fear that made her angry.

Mitchell would pretend to be concentrating on his sewing, and their mother would keep her eyes focused on her newspaper. Bruce was walking closer.

"If your mother wants Mitchell to go, he'll go." Bruce took his knee and thrust it against Laura's thigh.

It would leave a bruise for certain, but the impact didn't make a sound.

Finally, Laura had to tell someone. Not about Bruce. Not that. But about Jonas. She had to tell someone, and that someone was her best friend, Zan.

Zan had moved to town right smack in the middle of the school year, seventh grade, the year after Jamie Stein moved away. The teacher introduced the new girl to the class as Alexandra Benoit.

"It's Zan," the girl answered. "Not Alexandra."

"It says Alexandra."

"I prefer to be called Zan."

Laura sat back and watched, in awe of this skinny, orange-haired newcomer who was brave enough to correct the teacher.

"I think Alex is a more appropriate nickname for Alexandra."

"Zan. I'll stick with Zan."

At once Laura knew she had to become friends with this girl. She wasn't a rebel in the way Jamie had been, embracing the counterculture by wearing long skirts and headbands and no underwear. No, this girl was the real thing, a rebel with a cause. Besides, Laura was in the market for a new best friend.

.   .   .

"That's so crazy," Zan said.

"I know."

The girls were walking back to Zan's house from the grocery store. The sun was teasing the world, hinting at an early spring. Easter was still two weeks away, but Laura took off her hat and shook out her hair.

"No, I mean really crazy," Zan said. "He just disappeared?"

"I know."

"Well, you know, a love that isn't tested can't be real," Zan said. She poked her head into the paper bag, then her hand, and rummaged around. "Didn't we get bubble gum?"

"Where did you hear that? Anyway, jeez, I don't love him. I don't even know him."

"Well, maybe *he* loves *you*. So he's testing you." Zan found the gum.

"He doesn't love me. And I don't want to be tested. It was just really strange — that's all I can say."

They walked up the front steps of the trailer where Zan lived with her older sister, Karen — who, like Laura's brother, was absent most of the time, either physically or otherwise — her mom, and her stepdad.

"Nobody's home," Zan said. She pulled open the front door. "Come on."

Laura knew trailers weren't exactly supposed to be luxurious, but she liked it. It was compact and cozy. Everything had a place or a little pocket to slip into. The beds were attached to the floor, with drawers hidden underneath. Tables popped out of panels in the wall. Doors slid to the side and disappeared.

The living room wall-to-wall carpet was covered with a large shaggy rug. Laura plopped down on the couch. "Where is everyone?"

Zan turned on the television and fiddled with the antenna until a fuzzy picture appeared.

"My mom is at work. I have no idea where Karen is, but who cares?" she said. "And let's hope Pete never comes home." She slouched down on the shaggy rug and rested her head against the couch. Another thing that brought Zan and Laura together, or kept them together, was their mutual hatred for their stepfathers (in Laura's case, her mother's boyfriend).

"So, where were you going to go with him? Starburst?"

"Star*bucks.* I'm sure of it. I listened carefully."

"Well, let's call that number, then, like in the movie *Desk Set,* and find out what Starburst is." Zan sat upright.

"Starbucks."

"Whatever. Let's call."

"*Desk Set*'s a movie. That's not real."

"It is. That's what librarians do. They can answer any question you ask them. It's their job; they have to." Zan got to her feet. "Starbucks. It sounds like something futuristic, like *Lost in Space*. Or *Star Trek*. Do you think it's like something from *Star Trek*? Ooh, I love Dr. Spock."

"*Mr.* Spock. Dr. Spock is the baby doctor."

"Fine, let's call. The phone is in my mom's bedroom."

"We can't. That library from the movie was in New York City, remember? You can't make a long-distance call in the middle of the week," Laura said.

They ended up calling the Woodstock Public Library reference desk. Laura waited on the phone for ten minutes before she heard the librarian return and pick the phone up again. She sounded out of breath.

"From *Moby-Dick*?"

"From what?" Laura asked into the phone.

"Starbuck. From *Moby-Dick*."

"No, I don't think so. I think it has something to do with coffee. In New York City."

"Let me check again."

It was quiet on the other end, and then the librarian came back on the line.

"I'm afraid I can't find any reference to anything called Starbucks in New York City. Are you sure you have the spelling right?"

"Yes," Laura said, although of course she wasn't.

"The only thing I can find is a small coffee-bean company in Seattle, Washington, on 2000 Western Avenue. Does that help at all?"

"No, but thanks," Laura said, and she hung up the phone.

▢▢▢▢

SOMEHOW Jonas wasn't that surprised when Laura vanished as soon as they stepped off the train. It wasn't as if he was expecting it, but it didn't feel that out of the ordinary anymore. There was something so unordinary about being on that subway, the way it looked, the way people were dressed—kind of grungy, old-fashioned maybe. Of course, he wasn't really paying attention to his surroundings. Mostly to Laura. The doors had closed behind him, the crowd dispersed, and she was gone.

Jonas slumped down on a bench facing the tracks and just sat. It was a few minutes before he noticed someone was sitting beside him, a minute or two more before he recognized the guy from the museum.

Yeah, it was probably, almost definitely—it *was* the same guy from the Met. Wasn't it?

"What are you looking at?"

Jonas startled. "Uh, nothing." The boy was Hispanic and had a kind of ghetto look, but then again not really. He was wearing really high-waisted pants and a plasticky jacket. He had a ghetto *vibe* but an almost nerdy look.

"I mean, sorry," Jonas added. "I just thought I saw you at the . . . somewhere before."

"Seriously?" the boy asked. "I doubt it." He looked Jonas up and down.

"Yeah. There was an exhibit at the museum, I think."

The station was empty. You were supposed to be careful in New York, especially down in the subways, but Jonas didn't feel like being careful. He felt like finding out what had happened to Laura. Why she had run away. Why she had disappeared. And this guy seemed connected somehow.

"Oh, I thought maybe you were an artist," Jonas went on. "You know, a painter or something. The way you were studying that painting."

The Hispanic kid, the teenager, sat up straighter. "I am." He made a motion in the air with his hand, his finger bent. "A writer. I write."

"A writer?"

"You know. A writer."

"Oh," Jonas said out loud. The bent finger, the hand. He was holding a can, an imaginary can. "Oh, spray paint. A graffiti—"

The boy looked around. "Whoa there, man. Watch it."

Jonas lowered his voice. "So, what are you doing here?"

"Waiting," he said. "Watching. My train should be coming any minute. Unless they got to it early."

"*Your* train?" But as soon as he said it, Jonas figured it out. The Pink Panther, the train Laura had been on. "Oh, right. Cool. When did you do it?"

"Last night. I wanted to see it first thing this morning on the Jerome Ave. El when it first came out of the layup, but the cops were all over it. They don't expect us up here. You write?"

"Me? No."

" 'Cause I see you here, like you're benching."

"Benching?" Jonas was sitting on a bench, but benching? "No, seriously. I'm not."

"And the camera. I thought maybe you were somebody."

Jonas looked down at the bag strapped across his body. Not many people knew what it was. "Oh, well, yeah. I take pictures."

The boy reached inside his jacket and pulled out his camera. It was a film camera, an old Nikon FM series.

"Nice," Jonas said. "You shoot old school."

The kid smiled. "Old school? Man, who are you kidding? This is state of the art—" And the sound of the nearing train vibrated the station. "Whoa, brother. Get ready—here comes my train. You're going to read about me one day."

It wasn't the same subway car or the same artwork that he had seen the other day, but the style was consistent; the flare was the same. Like when you see a Monet and you know it's a Monet. No Pink Panther this time; it was a Christmas scene, snow and pine trees, a smiling Santa, and the name SPIKE—this boy's name, Jonas assumed—was written across the side of the car just below the windows in wild-style 3-D neon colors, and when the doors flew open, Laura was inside.

10

NOW. There. Here. It was Laura. Her clothes were different. She was wearing only a sweater when, before, though he wouldn't swear to it, wasn't she wearing a jacket, a coat or something? Her hair was pulled back, not hanging loose like it was before, but it was definitely her.

When she saw him, she stood up immediately, holding on to the bar, greeting him as he entered the car. "Where did you go?" she demanded.

"Where did *you* go?" Jonas asked. The door shut and the train lurched into motion.

"I didn't go anywhere," Laura answered. "I didn't even know where I was. I had to call my dad."

Jonas tipped his head down. "I'm so sorry. Right. You're not from the city."

"And my dad wasn't home," Laura went on. "I had to wait three hours until I could reach him, and he wasn't very happy."

Jonas laughed. "Three hours? What are you talking about?" The subway traveled on its route. It stopped and started again. Neither one of them got up to leave.

She was so pretty, even agitated and talking fast, her forehead crinkled up, and her hands moving around. Maybe more so. Prettier.

"I got in big trouble, you know. My dad was worried, and he got so mad. I mean, I don't think he was that worried, but he acted like he was. He even called my mom to see if I had gone back home, but my mom was at work and Bruce had to—"

Jonas was shaking his head. "Wait," he said. "Stop. What are you talking about? I just saw you, I don't know, twenty minutes ago. Tops."

Laura got very quiet.

"And weren't you wearing a different coat just before?" Jonas asked her, but he wasn't really asking a question, and slowly he stopped talking.

It took him a moment to breathe and settle into his seat. He had nowhere to go. The train would travel forward and then it would travel back, same car, same line, same station, as long as Laura was beside him. His heart wasn't thumping anymore. It was expanding. They sat on the subway, side by side, looking across at the empty seats. Jonas let his hand drop to his side. He felt for Laura's fingers and she didn't pull away. He felt something move through her hand into his, from his skin onto hers. He couldn't say what it was exactly, but it definitely didn't "suck."

THE love letters began to dwindle, and eventually, by around Christmas — well, Christmas for SongCatcher @gmail.com, according to the e-mails; Hanukkah for the Goldman family — the communications stopped altogether. By the time they ended, Jonas had collected 256 e-mails, sometimes sixteen a day just from his dad. Some with only a line or two:

> Go outside and look at the moon. It's amazing tonight.

And then less than a minute later:

> We may not be together but we gaze upon the same moon wherever we are. I think of you without rest.

God, please. Seriously?

Jonas became immune, as if they were written by other people, as if his mom were not in the kitchen making dinner, or out at her belly dancing class, or in the den giving Hebrew lessons, and his dad were not working late again, or getting in a cab on his way to the airport for another business trip.

He didn't read anything in the letters that told a story, anything that might explain why the number of e-mails tapered off and then ended for good. No, the letters were more like bad poetry, or soft-core porn, little innuendos and references to meetings they must have had together. Whatever terminated the relationship happened offscreen, out of Jonas's sight. It wasn't recorded on the Internet. Not for his eyes.

What *was* clear was the change in his father's behavior at home when it was all over. It was as if his parents were teenagers again. Even Lily noticed.

"Mommy and Daddy are kissing again," she said, and giggled.

Jonas looked up from his computer at his sister. She didn't know anything.

"So what," he snapped at her.

"They're in love," Lily sang. She stood at the doorway to Jonas's bedroom. "Like in the movies."

Yeah, just like that.

Lily was eight years old. She had long blondish hair

that hung in delicate, still-baby-fine banana curls, their mother's unabashed pride. Lily stood smiling widely, just under forty inches tall, about face level with the third drawer of Jonas's desk, where old underwear, too-small T-shirts, assorted single socks, and a stack of 256 e-mails that never should have been there lay patiently waiting.

They're not in love, Lily, he wanted to tell his little sister. *It's not going to last. Nothing does. It's not real.*

"Just like in the movies," he told his sister. "I know."

He watched her face brighten. She had felt it too, even if she didn't know what *it* was — the tension, the fighting, the distance between their parents. Now it was better. So, why not?

And if you had asked Jonas what he thought of love then, he probably would have laughed, or made a joke, or pointed out the naïveté of his little sister, who had her heart broken when their parents split for good only a month after that and SongCatcher reappeared on the scene as Lorraine, the girlfriend.

MAX'S parents met in traffic court on Fordham Road in the Bronx. The courtroom was packed with people waiting their turns, sitting quietly on the benches as cases were called up one by one.

"No talking, please." The bailiff was constantly pointing to people and telling them to be quiet.

"Want a book?"

David had turned toward the whisper. The girl was smiling and holding out a small paperback. He wanted to look down at the cover, to see the title, but this girl's face was so beautiful. She was clearly Spanish, dark eyes so dark he couldn't see the pupils, with long black lashes. Her hair was straight and it shone, even under the horrible fluorescent lights of the courtroom. Her front teeth were adorably crooked.

"Well, do you?"

It wasn't until she repeated her question that David realized he was staring.

"Thanks." He took the book she slid across the wooden bench. He wanted to ask her name. He wanted to marry her.

"Lowenbein." The bailiff called out the next case. He said it again, louder.

"Is that you?" the girl asked. "That must be you. No one else is getting up."

It was. By the time he was done, given a twenty-five-dollar fine and three hours of driving school, she was gone. David waited three weeks to finally open — but never did read — the book that was marked with a name and address: Idalia Rosario, 255 East 229th Street, New York, New York.

David knew where that was. She lived in the Edenwald Projects, right around the corner from where he grew up in Eastchester. And that's where he would find her, woo her, and despite his parents' concerns that she wasn't Jewish, marry her.

A year and a half later, August 14, 1957, Max Eduardo Lowenbein was born.

"I know this is going to sound really strange," Jonas began.

He seemed to hesitate. Laura squeezed his hand in comfort. She would have had no explanation for why she did that, for why she had let him hold her hand in the first place. In a world in which so little felt right, where visiting her dad, or being home with her mom and Bruce, just living every day, was something akin to traversing a field of land mines, this boy felt safe.

"Go on," Laura said.

The hum and shaking of the train were soothing. There were only a couple of other people in the car, and neither seemed to notice anything was strange or out of place. The placidity of these strangers felt calming.

"Have you ever heard of that word *beshert*?" Jonas asked her.

Laura shook her head.

Jonas inhaled and went on. "Well, it's a Jewish word. It means 'fate,' more or less. 'Meant to be,' but there's a lot more to it than that."

"I'm listening," Laura said.

Light suddenly flooded the car. How long had they been on the subway? The train was outside now, out of the darkness of the tunnels. It was traveling aboveground, above the city streets, on an elevated track. Laura turned to look out the window.

"Where are we?"

"Way uptown, the Bronx. We're on the El, almost the end of the line."

"What happens then?" Laura asked. She could look down and see — even through the layers of dirt and deep scratches in the glass — the streets, the buildings, people walking through their lives.

"It stops and then goes back the other way."

"Really?"

Jonas leaned closer. He was looking out the window too. His face right beside hers. Laura thought he might kiss her. She would have to decide whether to let him or not. But he didn't try.

"Really," he answered her, and he smiled like he thought her naïveté was cute. She hoped it was.

"They don't run as often late at night," he told her.

Laura shifted back onto the bench. It wasn't comfortable. It was a hard plastic. She could see garbage, wrappers, cigarettes, and gum tossed under the seat in front of them, but she wanted to stay. Now, here. She could breathe. Here on this grimy New York subway she felt whole. There was nowhere else she wanted to be.

"So, what more is there?" she asked him. Let the wholeness last. She wanted it to last.

"To what?"

"That word you said."

"Beshert."

Laura echoed. *"Beshert."*

They would stay in the car for another round-trip, from the Bronx to Brooklyn, from Pelham Bay Park to South Ferry. No one seemed to notice them, not the crowds getting on, clearing out, and filling again. Surely they didn't notice anyone else.

"It's not like I'm religious or anything," Jonas told her. " 'Cause I'm not. It's just kind of a neat story."

Did he really just use the word *neat?*

"So, what is it?" Laura asked. "The story. What is it?"

"Well, it's more like a myth."

"OK, what is the myth?"

Jonas knew the story from Hebrew school, a place he had dreaded going to, skipped as often as possible, and quit as soon as he was allowed. It was run by Chabad on the West Side, and while the students were as far from Orthodox as you could get, the female teachers all wore long-sleeved shirts, covered their heads with scarves or wigs, and were the most amazing storytellers Jonas had ever heard.

It went something like this:

Before you come into this world, while your body is floating safely inside the mother womb waiting to be born, your soul is introduced to its mate, your *soul* mate. This is your *beshert*. Before you are born, all knowledge of the universe is yours, so that when you meet this person on earth, you will be able to recognize him or her. However, for most people, the trauma of birth is so great, it causes nearly all that understanding to be forgotten immediately, and babies come into the world knowing nothing, completely helpless, and totally dependent. It takes a lifetime to regain all this knowledge, and most people never do. However, you will, again, cross paths with your soul mate on earth, and if you are lucky, a tiny glimmer of your memory will be triggered, and you will feel that you've known this person your whole life, even though you've only just met. The difference in your ages or where you lived or where you were born won't matter. You met your *beshert* outside of time and space as we understand it. You met your *beshert* in heaven, and though it is destiny that you meet again on earth, it will be your choice to stay and listen to your heart.

But that is not what he told Laura.

"I'm not sure," Jonas said. "I think it's Yiddish, actually. It means *destined,* like fate, you know?"

"So, that explains why you disappeared from the subway three weeks ago and now you're here?"

"I don't know, but something's going on," Jonas said. "I know I'd like to be able to see you again."

He could see Laura blushing, her face spotted with red at the top of both her cheekbones. He wanted to touch her skin. It looked so soft. He was sure it would be. He wanted to lean in and press his lips against hers.

"So, we can see each other again, can't we?" Laura said. She tilted her face down. He saw the part in her hair. "But I better get to my dad's now. What time is it, do you know?"

Jonas reached into his pocket for his cell phone.

"That's weird." It was on, but the time wasn't showing up: 00:00.

He had no bars. He never did down in the subway, but it always showed the time. Laura leaned over.

"What's that?"

"Are you serious?" But he knew she was.

"Laura," he started.

"What is that? A radio?"

Jonas looked up. There were a few people in the car with them at this point, and the next stop was Laura's, assuming she wanted to get to her father's. There was an African-American woman in a long, furry sweater and lots of blue eye shadow. There were two kind of nerdy-looking white men in stupid-looking suits and ties — nothing unusual there. And an old woman sat at the other end of the car, sleeping. Again, nothing unusual, except maybe that no one else was looking at a cell phone or BlackBerry or iPod. No one had earbuds or headphones on. Nothing unusual because everything about this was amazing.

He started again. "Laura —"

She jumped up. "Listen, I'm sorry. But this time I really have to go. I can't get in trouble again."

The train was slowing and jerked to a fast stop. The doors slid open and just before she bolted out, she bent down close to Jonas's face.

"I don't know what's going on either, but if you want, I think you can find me here."

She opened her mouth slightly; she leaned toward him; she pressed her lips to his. He hardly had time to return her kiss.

"I'll wait for you," he said, and she was gone.

.

11

IT would be another two weeks before Laura could get back to New York City, and this time Mitchell was with her. Zan would always ask what was happening, but Laura often didn't want to talk about it. When she got home, it felt as if it had never happened. It was almost easier to forget, like the end of the dream you are having that fades away as soon as you begin to wake up. All that's left is a vague feeling. Until she got back to New York, and the life behind her broke off and fell away like a snake sloughing its skin.

There had been no sign of Jonas anywhere. Laura was looking, intently, scanning every face on the subway, certain he was in another car, or just about to get on, or off. She even tried to find him in the throngs of people walking the sidewalks of Manhattan, more people than ever. The warm weather brought them out.

"You OK?" Mitchell asked her.

That was an odd thing, her brother inquiring after her. Their dad wasn't home from work yet, and the doorman had let them into the apartment.

"I'm fine," Laura answered. Mitchell had the TV on.

"You're so jumpy," he said. "What's going on?"

In a way, she wanted to tell him. There was a time when he was her older brother, a real older brother. They played TV tag and hide-and-seek; they filled water guns from the outdoor hose; they flew balsawood airplanes off the roof. The story goes that Mitchell even stopped a three-year-old Laura from running out into the street when they still lived in Brooklyn. He saved her life, the story goes.

"There's just something—" she started and stopped.

But it wasn't like that with Mitchell anymore. They had left Brooklyn Heights, left their dad, left TV-Wonder-bread-land and entered peace-marching-headband-wearing-tie-dye-world. And somehow, while Mitchell jumped ship, Laura was left standing on the other side, alone. She knew what it felt like to have the world gawk while you struggled. Mitchell didn't. He wouldn't understand. He was the secret police; she couldn't confide in him.

"I gotta go," she told Mitchell suddenly. She picked her jacket up from the couch.

"Where? What? No, you're not," Mitchell said, but he kept his eyes on *Sonny and Cher*.

Laura figured the best thing to do would be to return to the same subway station, maybe find the same train, the same car. Yes, she remembered the graffiti, the puffy letters, the Pink Panther or the snow-covered pine trees, and she found herself skipping down the stairs to the underground, afraid the train would come and she would miss it. Somehow missing it by only seconds would be so much worse than never knowing it had come and gone. She had no idea what to do other than walk forward and hope something would come to her, hope that when the time came to make a choice, she would know which was the right train. That's how it had happened before.

Two trains came by, both covered in messy, darkly scribbled lettering, the second with its windows whited out. But neither had the colorful three-dimensional tagging. When the third train hissed to a stop decorated with palm trees and beach umbrellas and the name Spike, Laura decided to just step on.

She couldn't wait any longer.

Maybe something would happen. She sat down on the first open seat and she waited.

Of course this could be a total waste of time, or worse. Mitchell could be calling their dad at this very minute, telling on her. What if her father called home again, and Bruce answered. But that wasn't really Mitchell's style. If push came to shove, Laura believed he would cover for her. There are some allegiances that rank above all others. Kids versus adults. And something told her to stay on this train.

The number of people in the car thinned out as the subway headed uptown. It was unusually hot. People were fanning themselves, trying to lower the stuck windows. The constant hissing of doors opening and closing, the bell that rang in warning, the vibration of the steel wheels, began to sound like a lullaby. Laura leaned her head against the wall. The heat, the vibrations. She felt woozy and she closed her eyes.

"I know you."

Laura's heart froze, her eyes flew open. You were not supposed to talk to strangers, anywhere, certainly not in New York City, and they weren't supposed to talk to you. But someone was talking to her. She sensed a male presence before she recognized his face.

"Spike?"

He stood without holding on to the bar, his legs splayed apart for balance but not so much that he looked like he was worried about falling.

"So, why are you here?" Spike asked her. "I mean, I know why I'm here. But why are *you*? This train goes to places no white girl should be." The bell sounded and the doors flew open. Spike moved toward them and waited.

Where was she? Had she fallen asleep and now she was lost? There wasn't even time to figure it out. The subway car was filled with people, not Midtown businesspeople but uptown people, hot and tired, all wanting to get home.

She felt so white and out of place. She knew she wasn't supposed to think this way, but she was afraid. Jonas hadn't shown up. She didn't know what subway she had even gotten on, where it went, or how to get back. The city was a huge web of underground danger, a maze she didn't understand, and Spike was the only face she knew.

"Wait!" Laura called out to him. There must be a reason she was here and he was here. But Jonas was not. Spike was about to leave.

"Wait, can you help me?" Then she said it again. "I'm looking for someone. Can you help?"

"OH, man. You don't know nothing about the Holocaust. You got it all wrong," he told her. "The people who survived weren't the strongest."

She was feisty—he'd give her that—so he had agreed to help her find this boy she was looking for. Max knew exactly who she was talking about. That boy who was separated from time and searching the tunnels, doomed to wander the earth for his sins, like Cain, though this boy had no such sins. He didn't belong here, in this time; that was for sure.

Max wanted his art to travel the same way, timelessly and forever, like that boy. The steel wasn't safe anymore. It was being buffed out every day now. It wasn't going to last, Max could feel it. Celluloid, that's where it was at. He needed to capture it, hold it. Film. That was the future.

They were riding the subway together, talking, just bullshitting, passing time, like he did with his crew. Only this was a girl, a white girl to boot.

"Of course they were the strongest, Spike," she countered. "Only the strong survive, don't they?"

"Max," he told her. "My real name is Max."

"I'm Laura," she said, and smiled. When she smiled, her face lit up and the sadness seemed to disappear, for a little while anyway. But it was worth it.

"So, then, who survives?" she asked.

"Well, not the strongest," Max said.

He wanted to help her. Really, he did. She was a searcher. He liked searchers. A truth seeker, like he was. You don't find them every day. But shit, she was really obsessed with the Holocaust. And she wasn't even Jewish. But she felt it, he knew. He could see it in her eyes. She was a seeker. And he wanted to help.

"The survivors were the ones with imagination," he told her. "They were the ones that never stopped believing."

She looked like she was buying it. Hell, it sounded pretty damn good, if he must say so himself. "Strength has nothing to do with it," he went on. "It was weakness. Weakness for food, and pretty clothes, parties, for the good old times, for love. It was the ones that could still dream. They were the survivors."

"For love?"

"Yeah, for love. Survivors are the artists, the painters, the writers," Max went on. "The dancers, the poets. The ones who can live in their minds while the rest of the world is falling apart."

They were on their way back again, after riding uptown to the very last stop, traveling in an unbroken line to Midtown, where she belonged.

"This is your stop," Max told her. Fifty-ninth Street. She'd figure it out from here.

"Well, I guess I should get off," she told him. She reached for her bag beside her.

"Sorry I couldn't help you find him," Max said.

"That's OK."

And then, wouldn't you know it, when the train stopped, that white boy was waiting for her, right there.

A goddamn fucking miracle, if you asked Max.

12

THE goal, of course, was to get a name for yourself. That's what *getting up* meant. A writer who has hundreds, *thousands,* of throw-ups, who has his name everywhere, all over a certain train line, is considered king of that line. But Max wanted more than that. He wanted to paint his masterpiece. He wanted people to talk about his work for years to come. He wanted them to remember him, not just for his name, but for his style.

In the future, they would write books and make movies about him. He had the talent, everybody knew that. He had already transformed the art of graffiti writing. When he first started, the lines were messy and flat, boring. Max had been the first one to move into 3-D, then into bubble style, filling in with fading colors. Practically no one was doing the fade when he started. Now, of course, you see it everywhere, but he was one of the first. Or so he said.

At the Writers' Corners, the one on 149th, they all wanted his tag in their black book. He was going to be famous and everyone knew it. He just needed to do something big, a whole car, end to end. He was almost ready. The weather was getting warmer, but not too warm. The 6 train was his target. He knew the route by heart. The One Tunnel was the ultimate layup. He had enough paint. The time was now, before he turned sixteen and could get in real trouble.

The MTA was all geared up about this new World Trade Center, but Spike was going to take the headlines; his burner would pull right into that station for the opening ceremonies next week.

It was going to be magnificent, and no one would ever forget.

JONAS woke up to his mother's crying. He slipped out of bed and knocked on her door as softly as he could, soft enough not to wake Lily but loud enough to be heard over her wretched sobbing.

Jonas heard his mother reach for a tissue, blow her nose, and pretend to be pretending nothing was wrong. "What is it, sweetie?"

"Mom, can I come in?" Jonas said through the door, although there was nothing he wanted to see less than his mother's blotchy, wet, swollen face. He didn't really want to see his mother in her bed. Before his dad left, his mother had never stayed in bed this long. Jonas had probably never been up before his mother in sixteen years. Now it was a daily occurrence.

"Certainly." She was wiping her face and pulling up the covers. The room still smelled of his dad's cologne.

Jonas sat down on the very end of his mother's bed, as far from her as he could. The shades were drawn, and it was dark. She used to get up and run Saturday mornings, rain or shine, all year long.

"Want me to make coffee?" he asked.

"That would be terrific."

Jonas stood up.

"I am so lucky. You're the best child any mother could ever hope to have. You know that, don't you?" his mother said.

Jonas didn't turn around. "Thanks, Mom," he said. It was like a cruel joke.

The good part was he could make the coffee, get Lily her cereal, plop her in front of the TV, and slip out of the house without having to explain anything to his mother.

He headed straight for the subway station at Fifty-ninth Street.

Jonas now knew he could find Laura, not what time but *where*. Always on the same subway, on the uptown 6 train, sometimes the downtown, *sometimes* being the operative word. It took all of waiting, hit or miss, sitting in the station, but it was always the 6 train, the one with graffiti. The train with the art-work, the mess, the letters, tags, pictures, and color splashed all over it.

Jonas never knew he'd have the train schedule so clearly mapped in his head. He knew the routes and pretty much the entire timetable. He flew down the stairs into the darkness of the subway station, eyes wide open, drinking in all the available light.

"You're not the falling-in-love type," Nick had told him.

"I know I'm not," Jonas agreed. For different reasons, they had both finished their math quiz early and were sitting in the faculty stairwell.

"Well, for someone who's not the type, you sure spend a lot of time thinking about her."

"And hanging out in the subway looking for her," Jonas added.

"You're shitting me! Is that where you've been? Is that why you never text me back?"

"No service down there."

Nick smacked his friend in the arm. "You still don't have her phone number?"

How could he explain? He couldn't. It didn't make sense. It sounded more than borderline crazy, so better left unsaid.

"You can't tie yourself down," Nick said. "This weekend. Saturday night. You and me. And you'll forget all about mystery girl with no phone."

It wasn't worth explaining, but Jonas had other plans.

Jonas swiped his MetroCard before he realized he had left the apartment without his camera, something he almost never did. He thought about going back, losing the fare, having to swipe his card again, but the uptown train stopped right in front of him. The graffiti had been scrubbed off and only the faintest outline remained, lighter in color than the rest of the metal car, a blurry outline of the huge puffy lettering. The windows were scratched but paint free.

Jonas stepped inside, expecting exactly what he found: Laura sitting, waiting, just as she said she would be.

"Sorry it took me so long," Laura told him.

Jonas lifted his brow. "So, how long?" It was Saturday morning now. It had been seven days.

The train jerked into motion.

But for Laura it had been longer, hadn't it?

He had figured it out. Somehow time was moving faster for her. Her kiss was still warm on his lips. He had seen her just last weekend.

He hesitated. "So, when *did* you see me last?"

"Me? See you? Don't you remember?"

She had no way to reach him. How many days had passed for her? How many weeks? No e-mail. No texting.

For a second he was seized with self-doubt, even jealousy for a world he knew nothing about and couldn't visit, much less control. What did she do with her time, the in-between time? But he shook off the feelings. He was so glad to see her again. Her face, her smile.

"It was two weeks ago, wasn't it?" she asked.

Jonas didn't answer.

Laura went on: "Yeah, as much as my mom likes to get rid of me, the bus from Kingston costs a lot and it's a long drive from Woodstock and we only have one car and it doesn't always start. My brother wasn't supposed to come with me, but after what happened last time, my mother made him . . ."

Jonas was only half listening. How could this

be possible? He interrupted her. "So . . ." he started slowly. "So, what year is it?"

"What year is it?" Laura echoed. "What year is it . . . when?"

"Now," Jonas said. "What year is it now?" He knew he was taking a risk. It sounded like a question from a science-fiction movie or one of the medical shows where the guy is waking up from a head injury. Laura must have been thinking the same thing.

"You want to ask me who the president of the United States is?"

Jonas didn't answer. He watched Laura's face, trying not to be distracted by the dip of her collarbones, the skin that was showing at her neck.

"You're serious, aren't you?" she asked him.

He nodded.

"OK," Laura said. She spoke more softly.

There were a few other people on the train. It was still pretty early.

"It's nineteen seventy-three," she began, and as she spoke, Jonas lifted his eyes and let them wander around the subway car, the greenish color of the walls, the molded plastic benches. He looked up at the print ad that decorated the top of the car, just under the rounded ceiling.

"And the president is—unfortunately still is—Richard Nixon," Laura went on. She seemed to be watching his face carefully. She spoke slowly. "But not for you, is it?"

Jonas shook his head. They both looked around the train. A youngish mother wearing lots of eye makeup sat with a sleeping toddler sprawled across her lap, and an older couple were holding hands at the other end of the train.

"Don't say anything," Jonas said.

"I won't."

They fell silent and let the train lull them for a while. The older couple got off. A tall man in a velour jogging suit got on.

"This is weird, isn't it?" Jonas said finally.

"Yeah," Laura said. "But it feels right."

IT did. Jonas hadn't felt this right in a long time. He had a sense of being home, right here in the subway car. And it was odd, since he had never liked being down in the subway system, being underground. When he was little, he was afraid the city would most certainly collapse on top of him. How can all those buildings and all those people and cars and buses be just eighteen feet above the tunnel? It was impossible.

"It's fine, Jonas," his father would say. "It's

perfectly safe. Look—" His father would take his hand and walk him down the steep concrete steps. The smell of urine and the roar of the trains would assault him.

"It's OK. Take another step. If you just *act* like everything's OK, it will be. Tell your body to just keep moving. Before you know it, it will feel just fine."

It seemed impossible, but Jonas trusted his father, and wouldn't you know it, like his father promised, the whole of New York City never collapsed into the ground. And now he was here with Laura, and it was safe again.

"So you live in Woodstock?" Jonas asked, metaphorically putting one foot in front of the other, acting as if everything was normal as Laura told him her story.

She told him about her mom and dad, about their move, about the changes, finally about Bruce. She had never told anyone about Bruce, she said. No one knew.

"You've got to tell someone," Jonas said. "That's against the law. What a sick bastard. You can't go back there."

"I live there," Laura said.

"Well, you can't." Jonas felt a rise in his heart, a fear, maybe, an urgency, a sense of indignation, and a powerlessness all at once.

Laura suddenly looked worried. The lovely calm fled her face. "I gotta go actually. I want to be back before my dad gets home. Is this the right stop?"

Jonas looked up. He hadn't noticed where they were. There was no electronic map on the wall above the straphangers' bar. He had no idea where they were along the route, only that they were heading back uptown again.

"I don't know. But you can't go. When can I see you again?"

"We've been managing so far," she said. She blushed. She actually blushed. Jonas felt his whole body rise with heat, remembering her mouth, her hands cupping his face when she kissed him.

He wanted more. This wasn't enough. It was crazy-making. "But what if I want to call you? What if you want to call me?"

"I guess we can't do that," she said. "But I'll come back. Will you?" She stood up.

His mind ran through the options: no texts, no phone, no e-mails. It was impossible to imagine. "But what if I can't wait?"

She scrunched up her face and shrugged, and there was that smile again, and there was the subway chime. The doors hissed opened. It was no use trying to follow, that much he had already figured out.

IT wasn't just their mom. Laura's dad insisted that Mitchell come into the city. He wanted to talk about something important, and he wanted to do it in person.

Laura's dad wanted to take her brother to Europe. It would be a business trip to West Germany that June. Then, after their dad had given the lecture he had been invited to present, they would travel. Once upon a time, perhaps their dad would have traveled Europe on a rail pass and stayed in youth hostels and studied the great artists, but as an art director, he gave talks on promotions and free giveaways. Still, it was a trip to Europe. Mitchell would have to miss the last week of school, but their dad was sure he could get permission; after all, the trip would be educational. How many seventeen-year-olds got to fly to Europe?

"But you'll have to cut your hair," Laura's father said. He had ordered Chinese food, and they were eating at the table. No TV this time — a discussion was on the agenda.

Mitchell put down his chopsticks. Laura and her dad ate with good old-fashioned utensils, but Mitchell insisted on chopsticks. He'd asked for brown rice, but the restaurant only had white, so he had made his own and carried it in with him.

"I'm not cutting my hair," Mitchell said.

Their dad put down his fork.

"What do you mean, you're not cutting your hair?"

It was perfectly obvious to Laura, predictable. Mitchell wouldn't cut his hair. If this conversation had occurred a few months ago, she would have been upset that her father hadn't even considered taking her, but now she was glad. She had only one thing on her mind, and it took up every space in her waking brain. She was hardly listening to them bicker.

"I mean, I'm not cutting my hair."

"You have to. It's not a choice. They won't let you into the country. You can't get a passport photo looking like a freak."

But Mitchell stayed oddly calm.

"Then I guess I can't go," he told their dad.

Oh, no. Not good. Their dad did not stay calm.

"I've had enough"—he raised his voice—"of this hippie crap. This is an opportunity of a lifetime, and you're not going to miss it because of some disrespectful teenage rebellion. You'll cut your hair."

"You're the one being disrespectful. This is my body, my hair. I'll do with it what I want. You can't tell me what to do. You can't turn me into some square, conservative, brainless automaton like you."

Laura pushed her chair away from the table. She wanted to hold on to the last particles of memory Jonas had left on her skin, on her lips. When the subway emptied out, on either the last or second-to-last ride from the Bronx to Midtown down toward Brooklyn and back, they had had a few moments alone. This time Jonas had pulled her toward him, reaching his arm around her waist.

She fit. Perfectly.

Into the curve of his arms and the space where his shoulder met his chest, like their bodies had once been connected. She remembered learning about the continental drift and looking at it for the first time on a map of the world. Ah, yes, of course anyone could see it, where South America would slip naturally into Africa, North America fit right under Europe, and Greenland nestled into Russia. Something had torn them apart and now they were together again.

He always acted as if he needed to know when he would see her again and couldn't bear not knowing when.

But what if I can't wait until next time?

If she brought her hair to her nose, Laura believed, she could smell him still nestled there.

"What the hell are you *doing?*" Mitchell asked her.

Their father had left the table in a huff. Laura ignored her brother.

Next time seemed so far away, not even on the horizon, but for the time being, *next time* made all of this so much easier.

13

"OK, so look her up," Nick was saying. "Google her."

Not like that hadn't occurred to Jonas right away.

Nick sat with his finger poised above the keyboard. "What's her last name?"

"Like I'm going to tell you."

Jonas was babysitting his sister, a gift to his mother, who had a date Saturday night. An enormous gift, according to Nick, who was keeping him company. She promised to be back early. Most likely before ten, his mother said.

"Stay out, Mom," Jonas had told her. "Have a good time."

"Ten thirty the latest," she promised.

Enough time to hit the subway when she got back.

"OK, then, let's go find her. I think it's about time I met this girl," Nick suggested. "C'mon. Lily would love it, a little field trip."

"Are you kidding?" Jonas was cleaning up from dinner, chicken parmesan, picking off cheese stuck to the plates, while Nick sat at the counter with the laptop.

"I'm not. Or you can give me her last name and *I* can Google her. Nineteen seventy-three? Hell, she's probably over fifty years old now, right? Sounds hot to me."

Jonas nearly regretted telling Nick anything—about Laura, about the strange vintage-looking subway car, the wild, colorful graffiti, and about the even stranger shift in time, how what was apparently days or even weeks for Laura could be a matter of minutes for Jonas. He had no idea.

Oddly, their time together seemed out of time completely, neither night nor day, present nor past. The subway car itself was a constant, but the way minutes passed, or hours, the way they didn't at all, was hard to figure out and hardly mattered.

Still, telling Nick might have been a mistake.

But Nick hadn't laughed. And he hadn't doubted what seemed impossible.

"Sorry," Nick said quickly. And he was sorry, again. "But we *could* Google her and maybe we'd find out where she lives, or lived. I mean, lives now. Or then. I mean — you know what I mean."

"Forget it. The Internet is the source of all evil," Jonas said. "E-mails can be big trouble."

"You don't know her last name, do you?"

"No."

"I don't think Googling 'Laura, Woodstock, New York, 1973' will give us much. Are you certain it's New York? There's a Woodstock in Vermont, you know."

"I'm sure," Jonas answered, but of course, he wasn't. He wasn't even sure it was still 1973 for Laura.

Nick let out a sigh. "This is clearly a no-win situation, my friend. How do you know she's telling the truth? Honestly, I think you might be driving yourself crazy. I think your guilty brain is getting the better of you."

"What guilty brain?" Lily walked through the living room and up to the kitchen counter.

If it was no accident that his father had left his e-mail open on the computer, it was less of an accident that Jonas had printed them out and his mother found them. But in that moment, Jonas regretted having confessed any of that to Nick. Telling on himself hadn't made him feel better anyway. And now it was going to come back and bite him in the ass.

She said it louder. "What guilty brain?"

"Nice work," Jonas said. Lily was a hard one to dissuade. When she got something into her skull, she rarely let go. Over the years, bribery and promises had only made it worse.

"*What* guilty brain?"

"Nothing, Lily. Go back and watch TV."

"There's nothing on. When's Mom coming home? Where did she go? What guilty brain?"

"Nothing on? With five hundred channels? Netflix? You must have something on the DVR." Jonas knew he sounded like their mother. Or Nick.

"It's about Mom and Dad, isn't it? The divorce, isn't it?" Lily said.

Nick looked over at Jonas, and Jonas wished he hadn't. Lily was fishing. She didn't know anything. But it was too late.

"I knew it," Lily burst out. "You know what I did. You know it's my fault." And she started crying.

"Oh, jeez, what's happening?" Nick had two older brothers, and this crying stuff made him nervous. Jonas told him to go home.

"It's fine. I'm not mad at all. I'll talk to you later,"

Jonas told him. He pushed his friend out the front door.

"I'm really sorry." Jonas could hear him on the other side.

"It's fine," Jonas shouted.

He finally got Lily to stop crying and go to bed, only by assuring her he would never tell their mother about how she broke the hand mirror in the bathroom, though he had been completely unsuccessful in trying to convince her that the broken hand mirror had nothing to do with their parents splitting up. Somehow Lily had come to believe that directly after her mother found the broken mirror — and Lily flatly denied having anything to do with it — her parents had ended up fighting. And then ended up getting divorced, and somehow Lily connected it all to the lie, and the mirror, and to herself.

It was a story, her story, just like any other story, as plausible as it was implausible. Most people will tell themselves anything in order to feel better about themselves, but some people do the opposite. Lily was truly her brother's sister. For the briefest moment as her sobs took over her body, Jonas (thinking that surely no one had enough liquid stored inside to remain alive after crying so long) considered telling his sister that it was his fault, not hers. But then, as quickly as she had begun crying, she stopped and she fell asleep, most likely from sheer exhaustion and dehydration. And he never said anything.

"How was it, Mom?" Jonas asked because he wanted things to be all right—if not better than before, at least right enough.

"It was awful, Jonas," his mother told him. She dropped her keys in the bowl by the front door. "People just lie, all the time. Is Lily asleep?"

He nodded.

"I'm going to bed. Lock up, will you, sweetie?"

"Sure, Mom." When she was in her bedroom, Jonas took his keys, grabbed his camera bag, and closed the door behind him.

MAYOR Lindsay had declared war, and by early 1973, well over fifteen hundred New York City youths had been arrested for vandalism. He called graffiti "demoralizing and obscene," and he said the graffiti writers were "insecure cowards" seeking recognition, though nothing could have been further from the truth.

There was talk of making spray paint illegal for anyone under eighteen, not only to purchase but to be found carrying. Attack dogs were brought into the yards, and coils of razor wire were added to the tops of the fences. Not only did MTA guards, who were usually too lazy or too fat to chase anyone for very long, patrol the yards and layups, but now real New York City police were put on "graffiti duty," and the cops didn't like it. It had always been risky sneaking into the yards at night to work, but now it was down-right dangerous.

Max was thinking of changing his tag name again.

THE city looks purple at night. The streetlights catching the exhaust from the buses and taxis and cars, the headlights from all that traffic, the hot steam escaping from the sidewalk grates all rise up to the moon— when it's out and not totally blocked by the tall build-ings. The light is unnatural and filtered, not quite yellow anymore, not gray, but more purple. Jonas held his camera in his hand as he walked, adjusting the settings. He had never found Laura this late before. Most of their meetings, if you could call them that, had been during the day, at least on her end of things, on her way to or from her father's apartment as she explained it. She didn't go out at night, and she wanted to be back before dark. From what he could gather, the city must have been more dangerous back then, or maybe it was the fact that she wasn't a native. What time it was for Jonas didn't seem to affect anything.

Finding Laura was hit or miss. Jonas could ride the subway for hours and not see her all day, or go out Saturday morning first thing and there she was. Or sneak out late at night. There was no telling when she might appear, and it was killing him.

So when Jonas saw the kid from the museum, the writer, as he called himself, standing at the top of the subway entrance smoking a cigarette, he half expected to see Laura again right behind him, coming up the stairs.

Jonas was about to say something to him. *Spike, right?* But the kid spoke first.

"Hey, you're that boy," Spike said. "The *boy*friend."

"Huh?" Jonas managed. He looked down the stairs. Only a man bumping an oversize suitcase onto each step up into the light appeared from below. No Laura, though he could feel her. It was a longing. It never left him.

"She's not up here," Spike said. He blew smoke circles into the air. "She can't be. You know that."

Jonas didn't question how or why this kid knew that or why he should believe him, but of course he did.

"I don't know what she sees in you," Spike went on.

This kid had no right, no reason, to judge. *What did he know? Who the hell was he?*

"But if you do me a favor, I'll help you find her." He stamped out his cigarette on the sidewalk.

Jonas looked at Spike. It *was* Spike, wasn't it? He felt stupid using that name. That couldn't be his real name. On the other hand, Jonas was game for anything that could make it easier to find Laura.

"What do you want?" he asked.

"I need someone to take photographs for me. I need to record this. I need a record of it. I need witnesses to my greatness."

None of this sounded very safe. Why did this Hispanic kid need to ask a stranger to take a picture of his greatest if there wasn't something criminal involved? Just thinking that made Jonas feel like a racist, but on the other hand, better safe than sorry. He could practically hear his mother's voice.

"Why me?"

"Your camera." Spike nodded at the bag slung over Jonas's shoulder. "You've got a camera."

"I thought you had a camera," Jonas said. "I saw you with a camera before."

"It got stolen." Spike shook his head slowly. "So, you in, Romeo?"

The sidewalk lit by neon pouring from the storefronts, the traffic speeding to make the green light, the street lamps that bent their heads and illuminated everything below—nothing was different, maybe, from when Laura made her way to this subway station. But maybe everything was different—the make of cars, the way people dressed, the tensions, the dreams, the politics—he didn't really know. In the end it was the same concrete under his feet, and hers. The same black sky cut between the same soaring buildings; the same moon, just a different light.

"I can't wait all night," Spike said. "But, hey, if you're a chickenshit, I'll understand."

He was. Jonas had been pretty much all his life, but if he was going to see Laura again, he would have to think outside the box. Of course, that was understood. Lately nothing fit inside the box.

"OK, I'm in," Jonas said.

Spike nodded in approval and laid out his plan: the time, the place; it all came out fast.

"And don't forget"—Spike was still talking—"plenty of film, fast—four hundred or higher. No flash. You got a light meter? Be there. Don't forget. And I'll make sure she's here."

14

THE truth was, Max had no idea how to find that girl Laura and he certainly couldn't promise he'd bring her to Jonas tomorrow night or any night. He unlocked his closet. His mom didn't pry into his stuff, but he kept it locked anyway, and the key hung from a split ring holder that he attached to his belt loop. Max had work to do. This was art. True art is more important than love. It certainly lasts longer. He opened the closet door.

The shelves were stocked with spray paint, all colors. There was Red Pepper Red and Cherry Red. He had to know which one to choose. There was

Golden Pear Yellow and Bright Idea Yellow, very different. Celery. Hosta Leaf. Global Blue or Peekaboo. Rich Plum and Purple. It had taken him months to collect it all. It had to be lifted, not bought. It just did. He didn't make the rules.

If his father knew he had stolen all this paint, shoplifted anything at all, he would kill him. His dad had wanted to move for years. Out of the Bronx. To Yonkers, he would say. Westchester somewhere. Or Connecticut. But Max's mother wouldn't leave her family. Her mother, Max's grandmother, was housebound. She needed her family nearby. His mother called him for dinner again.

Max stuffed the cans he needed into a suitcase, and more into his pockets, to see how many he could carry. Then, carefully, he put them all back, arranged in order according to hue, and locked the closet door.

"Max," his mother shouted down the hall. "Did you hear me?"

He ignored her for a little longer and sat down with his notebook to work out the exact numbers. He had measured the cars, the windows, the doors, everything. He had drawn a grid and sketched out his drawing, square by square. He would need fillers to get it all done in one night, but he knew a couple of younger kids dying to follow him.

"Max. Now."

Max shut his notebook. He was hungry anyway. He would be ready by next weekend. Next weekend. He would be ready.

SHE wasn't there — at midnight exactly — at the train station. Spike was there, or whatever his name really was, but no Laura.

"I'm telling you, man. I can do it. Something's happened, that's all. Just be patient."

"This is such bullshit," Jonas told him. They were already on the train, riding uptown, all the way to the end of the line. Never a good idea for a white Jewish boy in the middle of the night. It had been hard enough getting out of the house without arousing suspicion, especially without Nick, who texted him pretty much all night long. It required a series of typed lies, all of which he would probably be caught in tomorrow morning.

"What's your real name?" Jonas said. "Just fucking tell me." They were the only ones in the car. Another bad sign.

"Max Lowenbein," he said. "There. You satisfied? Now, will you just take the pictures?"

"Lowenbein?" Jonas said. "You're Jewish?"

"Yeah, so what?"

Jonas rested his back against the hard plastic seat. The train was littered inside with black graffiti. He wondered why he hadn't noticed that before. "Nothing. I just thought you were Hispanic."

"You think there aren't any Puerto Rican Jews?"

Jonas had never heard of that, but of course he knew there were Spanish Jews. He had learned his history — Sephardim, Marranos, the Inquisition — more Hebrew school memories.

"Cool," Jonas said. "So am I."

"No, duh."

"Really?" Jonas asked. It was that obvious?

"Really."

Maybe this was all crazy and Laura certainly wasn't going to be here, but it was exciting in a way Jonas had never felt before. Scary and different, and he felt very much alive. He had that same feeling of being beyond time, in a space in between. People always talked about how teenagers thought they were immortal, that a part of their brains had not fully developed and they couldn't understand consequences. Jonas had never been very daring, never got in much trouble, didn't drink or smoke very much. So maybe this is what daring felt like. Maybe it was about time.

The train ended its run for the night at the top of the Bronx at Pelham Bay Park. Max told Jonas to stay close. They exited the train with the last few remaining passengers and then slipped down onto the tracks and pressed their backs against the wall.

"Watch out for the third rail," Max whispered. "And the rats."

"Holy crap."

It was darker than any darkness Jonas could remember. His heart was pounding.

"But if you feel one, don't scream," Max said. "Just wait. And keep quiet."

They listened as the conductor shouted some instructions. The doors were locked; the train began to move slowly.

"Grab on." Max stepped up and grabbed on to the back of the train, holding the bars and perching his feet on the narrow platform that jutted off the end. "Hurry up."

In that way, they made their way to the layup and began their work. It turned out that Max had over twenty-five cans of spray paint packed in his suitcase. He wanted Jonas to document the entire project. He wanted it witnessed, recorded. *If you don't tell the story, it might as well never have happened.*

"It's going to be the biggest piece this city has

ever seen," Max said. He began with an outline—huge, thick black lines. It was clear he had it planned out to the last dot, the last fill. Where he would start, how he would finish.

"What's a 'piece'?" Jonas had his camera out. The lighting was fantastic, an eerie overhead single bulb. They were underground in an area of the tunnels that Jonas had never seen before. Fencing had been erected along the concrete sides. There were no benches, no signs, no ticket booths or turnstiles, just trains resting on their tracks and darkness.

"My masterpiece, man. My Sistine Chapel. My *Birth of Venus*. My *Twelfth Night*. My *La Gioconda*."

"Man, you know your art history." Jonas checked his meter. He set the aperture as wide as he could and the shutter speed as slow as he could. "Hold it, don't move so much. Let me get you in the shot with all this paint."

Jonas used up one whole roll in the first ten minutes. Max worked fast. Some shots would be blurry, streaks of color and movement. They might come out great. It was exciting.

Max sprayed with one hand, holding on to the upper bar above the windows and balancing his feet like a professional mountain climber about to rappel from a cliff. Hanging by his arm, he turned to look at Jonas. "Get this. It's my new tag. You like it?"

"I can't read it." Jonas took a few steps back. He checked his light meter again and knelt down for the shot.

"Can you read it now?" Max asked. "You've got to be able to read it."

"Yeah, I see it. Zippo? Like the lighter?"

"Yeah, that's me. Did you get it?"

"Yeah, I got it." Jonas lifted the camera to his eye. It would be a great photo.

"So, why is this chick so important?" Max jumped down.

Jonas was about to say something about Laura. He didn't know why, why he would ever confide in this kid, but he wanted to talk — about himself, his family, even his father, maybe especially about his father — but he heard someone shouting, a male voice.

"Oh, shit. Cops! We gotta run."

"What?" Jonas snapped on his lens cap. He dropped his camera back into his bag and flung it over his head and across his shoulder.

"Grab your shit. We gotta get outta here."

Lights, like an airport runway, illuminated the layup. Max was about fifty feet ahead already, running down the tracks. The farther away he got, the harder he was to make out in the darkness. Jonas took off running after him. His legs burned as if he had been running for miles already. His heart raced faster than he had ever felt it before. He could hear the police behind them, close enough that to keep running seemed the best option.

"Where's the spot? It's here somewhere. Damn, where's that hole?" Max was reaching around in the darkness, his hands groping along the chain-link fence. "It's here. I know there's a spot you can lift up."

Jonas felt the lights getting closer. He considered just giving up, explaining the whole thing.

"Got it!" Max slipped low to the ground and pushed his way through the fence. "C'mon."

Jonas followed, and so did the heavy footsteps, the shouting. "We got you, motherfuckers!"

Max reached the grate on the ceiling that would bring them to street level and pushed upward. "It's closed." He pushed. "It's jammed! Holy shit. Holy crap."

"Jump!" Jonas said. It was high, but they could do it. There was that game machine at the NBA store on Fifth Avenue that Jonas and Nick always used to go to. It measured your standing jump. For one day, Jonas had held the highest jump record for his height. He needed it now.

"One . . . two . . . three . . ." Jonas called out. Together they leaped up and kind of punched their fists into the grating. Dust and dirt came down on their heads as it gave way, and just as the lights crept up over their feet, they climbed out onto the street. There were a few people standing there as they exited the tunnel, dirty and bleeding from their knuckles, but they didn't stop.

Jonas ran like he had never run before in his life. He had no idea which way or where he was going. Ten minutes must have passed before he dared to slow down and stop. He doubled over, leaning on a mailbox. He looked up to see what street he was on — 179th Street and Sedgwick Avenue — and saw that he was alone.

ZAN asked Laura if she believed in reincarnation.

"Because my sister does, you know. Karen does. It's part of all that hippie-Indian-Hindu stuff she's into. That's what you're smelling," Zan said. "She burns it all the time. It's incense."

"I like it." They sat on the floor of Zan's bedroom. It had been four weeks since Laura had gone to visit her dad. There was no real explanation for that, but then again, Laura had learned not to ask too many questions.

"She's meditating so she can come back as a guru

or an elephant or something. That's the reincarnation thing."

Laura knew what she meant. Her mom and Bruce had a series of large, colorful posters in their bedroom. If you didn't look closely or were far away, at first they almost looked like friendly Saturday-morning cartoon characters. Most were women, with very white, almost dusty-white, skin, wearing yellow or pink or turquoise flowy skirts and bikini tops. Some were half human, half animal, and brightly colored with big eyes. Her mother had explained that each poster was of a different god representing some aspect of the Hindu belief. Laura had learned in school about the Hindu caste system and that Hindus believed in reincarnation as a way to return to earth as a higher incarnation, each time more enlightened.

"But I think she burns the incense to cover up the smell of the reefer," Zan went on. "And notice it's constant."

The musk or ylang-ylang or whatever was the undertone to the stronger skunky odor.

"It's not working." Laura laughed. The whole trailer, in fact, reeked.

"She says getting high helps her when she meditates on her past lives," Zan said. "So she can become enlightened and come back as John Lennon's girlfriend. Even though she's got Dennis Porter in there with her now."

According to Hinduism, after the death of the body, souls go either to heaven or hell depending on their deeds on earth, but they do not stay. They go there to either enjoy or suffer, but in both cases, they learn their lessons and return to earth to try living their life over again.

"All I know is that there was some horrible mistake in letting Bruce come back as a human being," Laura said.

Zan smiled. "Bruce will come back as a slug. I'm going to come back as Paul McCartney's girlfriend."

They rested their backs against Zan's platform bed, their legs stretched out in front, almost touching the wall. The tiny window above Zan's bed was open, and a small fan was blowing, but it hardly made a difference in the early summer's stifling heat.

"So, how about you?" Zan asked.

"What?"

"Are you a Paul girl or a John girl? Or a George girl? Because no one is a Ringo girl?" Zan went on. "Oh, are you a Ringo girl?"

Laura shrugged. She felt bad, not telling Zan she had seen Jonas again, kissed him, in fact. But it was her secret, and if she could keep it to herself, she was more able to believe it was true. No less, no more real than pretending to have one of the Beatles for a boyfriend.

Lying by omission was easy, though it probably meant a hundred years in Hindu hell and returning as a slug.

"My dad wants to take Mitchell to Europe with him," Laura said, changing the subject. "But Mitchell won't cut his hair. So my dad won't take him."

"Maybe he'll take you instead."

"Maybe," Laura said. "But I really don't want to go."

They sat quiet for a long while. Then a booming bass from Karen's room vibrated the walls, thumping steadily.

"Now she's screwing Dennis Porter," Zan said. She tried to keep a straight face, but they both ended up laughing.

"Hey, wanna do something dumb?" Zan said. "Something dumb and fun? Wanna play Mystery Date?"

"Oh, God. Really? Sure," Laura said. "You still have that game?"

They turned around and scooted back so Zan could slide a drawer out from under her bed. "Somewhere in here." She rummaged around with her hand. "I think I got it."

The box was a little bent, the cover flattened, but there it was, Mystery Date. The girls pictured were on one side of the door, the men on the other, all waiting to be perfectly matched up, as long as you had the right outfit.

Meet your secret admirer, it said at the bottom of the cover. Laura knew she already had.

15

THEN Jonas's father just showed up.

Ever since they'd bumped into each other in the subway, he had called every week, sometimes twice, and left messages. Jonas was considering changing his cell phone number, but he wasn't sure how to do that without his mother finding out, and it would probably cost money anyway. His father had taken to trying to block his number or calling from somewhere else, hoping, Jonas assumed, that his son would answer the call.

Instead, Jonas let any restricted number or number he didn't recognize go to voice mail. Sometimes he listened to the message; sometimes he just deleted it without listening. So Jonas was totally unprepared to find his father waiting for him outside his mom's apartment the following Saturday night on his way to the subway. It had been a month since he had last seen Laura, though he had made many trips to the underground and had lots of undeveloped film to prove it. *Tonight,* Max promised.

Yes. No, this was the worst possible timing.

It wasn't that Max hadn't promised every weekend for a month that she'd be there. Jonas had long since figured out that Max really had no clue whatsoever but tonight Jonas had a feeling. It was kind of funny when he thought about it. Jonas had had a crush on a girl a few years ago, in seventh grade, Sarah Metcalf. She was taller than he was, but it hadn't stopped him from dreaming. Jonas went online and searched everything he could about her, about her family, to find any bit of information that would stand in for spending actual time with her, since that seemed far out of his reach. He read about her father, who worked on Wall Street. There was an article published in 2009 about some shady dealings that did or did not occur. He read her name in an article about her third-grade travel soccer team, when they played in Central Park on some historic field on some historic day. He even Google-mapped her neighborhood on the East Side for no reason at all except that it made him feel like he was doing something toward getting to know her.

He knew nothing about Laura, not even her last name, and yet he felt more connected to her than to his own family. She had already entered his dreams, speaking to him, spending time with him, leaving an imprint like a memory. Of course Jonas had dreams about his mother and father and Lily, but not even Nick showed up in his dreams, and they had been friends for nearly eight years. And now here was his father coming out of nowhere just when Jonas had somewhere to go.

"Son?"

Jonas stopped. He hadn't even seen his dad coming. He must have been across the street, waiting, and hurried over when he saw Jonas leaving the apartment. It was 11:46. Jonas was in a rush.

Son? Was he kidding? Jonas's father never called him *son*. Nobody called their son *son,* except on those old shows that aired on TV Land that he and Nick liked to watch when they were stoned.

"I can't talk, Dad," Jonas said.

His father touched his arm. "It's late. You shouldn't be out. Nothing good goes on after midnight in New York. Does your mother know you've left the apartment?"

He knew what his father was thinking: drugs, clubbing, drinking, boosting cars, getting into fights, all bad things he had read somewhere that teenage boys might be involved in. It would never occur to him to ask, to ask and find out. To care.

"I don't have time for this." Jonas pulled his arm back. It scared him, actually, to have so much power, or rather to see his father with none.

When had this happened?

"You do and you will," his father said. "I've been calling you. I decided to just come over. I deserve some answers."

His father must have realized that was the wrong thing to say, but it was too late.

Jonas snorted. Without being totally aware of it, he lifted his chest and stuck out his chin.

"You deserve shit."

His father backed down, but he didn't give up. "All right. You want to be a man. I deserve shit, but what do you deserve? You think your mother needed to see those e-mails? You think that was brave? You think that was tough?"

Jonas felt a knife pierce his stomach, his heart, his eyes, his brain, all at the same moment, a million little cuts throughout his body.

"You don't know anything about life. You're a kid," his father went on. "I'm not saying I was right, and I'm not saying you were wrong. But there are many shades of gray in life, and you won't last long believing in the black and white."

Jonas couldn't think of what to say. He just wanted out of there. He wanted to find Laura before everything he had inside leaked out from those millions of tiny wounds.

"Screw you, Dad."

THE crafts fair lasted all weekend, and Laura's mother wanted everyone to go—Mitchell, Laura, and Bruce—to help man their table. They were trying to sell thick ceramic peace signs, tied with a bulky leather cord, meant to be worn as necklaces. They were Bruce's contribution, their ticket into the capitalist industrial complex. The rest of their wares were from a store in town called Hapiglob where Laura's mother worked. It sold leather clothing, leather accessories, and leather jewelry. She often brought home vests, pants, shirts, and jackets that still needed colored-glass beads threaded onto each piece of fringe. Laura's mother was being paid to sell at the fair and she also got a percentage of everything the store sold.

There had been crafts fairs in town before, but

no one had ever really seen anything like this. It was huge, with rows and rows of tables, booths, even tents, displaying the work of artisans and artists and craftspeople of all kinds. There were pottery and stained glass, and jewelry in gold, silver, and every other medium. Basket weavers, people who sewed quilts, people who made kaleidoscopes. Soap makers, candle makers, bread makers. It was a hippie mecca, except everything had a price. Even the peace signs.

Her mother had said she couldn't go to New York City this weekend, she needed Laura home to work the crafts fair, but she soon sent her out of the booth. Bruce was getting edgy and irritable. They weren't selling enough. Best stay out of his way.

Laura walked around, in between the rows. It was a cool but fiercely sunny day. She let herself daydream about Jonas. What would he think of this? Of tables made of tree stumps with branches for legs? Of sheepskin coats? Tie-dye everywhere, even baby clothes and men's ties, all for sale. And what would he say about a booth filled just with bumper stickers?

Fighting for Peace Is Like Fucking for Virginity.
War is not healthy for children and other living things.
Smoke Dope.
Hell no, we won't go.

Everything could be summed up as a slogan.

She couldn't wait to tell Jonas about everything she was seeing. She took it all in as if it were new, as if she could see it through his eyes and share it with him. She wanted to share everything with him—good, bad, funny, sad. Telling him made it real. Imagining what she would say, how she would say it, how he might respond, made her hopeful. Happy.

She couldn't wait to tell him about the photographer she saw, the one selling black-and-white portraits, selling a picture of *her.* She stared at the photograph so she could remember to tell Jonas all about it. It was taken three years ago. She hardly looked like herself at all, but she knew it was. Of course she knew it was. She had denied her own identity when the photographer recognized her.

"No, that's not me," Laura said. It was her image. It belonged to her, not for sale. There were American Indian tribes that believed a person's soul was taken if someone photographed them.

Laura's soul was not for sale. She knew Jonas would understand.

There were people selling macramé plant holders and Earth Shoes. She imagined describing for Jonas how ugly Earth Shoes were. She hardly knew him, yet she wanted to tell him everything, to be with him, more than anything she had ever wanted before.

The longing she hadn't even known she felt, would be filled. When she was with Jonas, she felt whole, complete. Fear, loneliness, emptiness, were gone, and if she could only be with him again, Laura knew she would want for nothing.

AT DUSK, Bruce packed up their wares and they piled into the car. Mitchell tried to get Laura to squeeze into the small compartment behind the backseat of their VW bug, the way she had when she was little, knees bent and slipped in like a suitcase, but she didn't fit back there anymore. Mitchell and Laura had to sit right next to each other, boxes of unsold ceramic peace signs between them.

In total, they had made twenty-two dollars and spent more than that on gas and food. Bruce was in a bad mood, and he drove fast, as if to prove how upset he was.

"I can drive," Laura's mother said.

Bruce kept his eyes straight ahead, raised his hand, and gave her the finger.

At her mother's request, they pulled into a rest stop off the highway.

"I've got nothing at home and the kids are starving."

Laura had been hoping for a McDonald's, where she knew over one million burgers had been served, and presumably that number would change when she ordered her hamburger to over one million and one burgers sold. Instead, they walked into a one-story building that looked like it had once been someone's home, with a sign out front that read GLORIA'S EATERY.

"No drinks. Just water," Bruce warned them.

Laura didn't like that they'd have to sit at a small table, so close. Bruce would have to sit either next to her or across. He ended up across, but one person down. Mitchell sat directly facing Laura, his eyes glassy and bloodshot. He ordered a cheeseburger and a milkshake. Laura was just happy to not be having seaweed. Her open-faced turkey sandwich was smothered in brownish gravy and came with a hefty serving of canned peas. It was delicious.

When it came time to leave, Bruce waved to the waitress. "No, just a check," he told her. When she started to walk away, he called her back. "Oh, and can we . . . ?" He looked around the table. "Can we have a doggie bag, please?"

Bruce pointed to Laura's plate, where she had left half a piece of soggy white bread that she was about to finish. The waitress gave him a funny look but shrugged and whisked the plate away.

As soon as she had backed into the kitchen, Bruce stood up. "Let's go," he said.

"What?" Laura's mother asked, but she got to her feet, most likely because Bruce was pulling on her arm.

"Cool," Mitchell said.

They were halfway to the exit when the waitress appeared, stepping out from the kitchen. She looked right at Laura at first, with a confused look on her face and then anger.

"I knew we never should have waited on you freaks," she said. She held a white paper bag in one hand, a check in the other.

"Clark!" she called into the kitchen. "Clark, get out here! Quick! Those hippies are skipping out on the bill."

Laura turned and ran out the door.

THE train had been newly scrubbed, it was obvious, but by the time it pulled into the 59th Street station, some writer had already motion-tagged it, writing on it as it traveled. Then the bright blue-and-green block letters spelling Zippo floated along the side, just under the windows, as the train came to a stop. This was the right train. He'd made it. Trying to forget his unpleasant encounter with his father, Jonas checked his cell phone. 12:05 a.m., and the doors slid open.

Laura was standing just inside the car, illuminated like a window display.

"Jonas." She whispered his name and he moved beside her.

For a long moment, they stood together, not moving, until the train pitched and Laura stumbled forward. Jonas held the pole with one arm and with the other pulled her into his body. She felt like she melted against him, and she let out a strange, feral-sounding cry.

"What is it?" Jonas shifted himself back so he could see her, but Laura wouldn't lift her face from his chest. "What's wrong?"

"Nothing," Laura said.

He pulled her body away from his so he could look into her face. "Listen," he said. "I can't do it like this. I can't do this. I need to know your last name. I need this to be real. I need to find you."

They sat down on the seat. "You can't," Laura said. "It's too crazy. It's too creepy weird. If you found me, I'd be really old. *Really* old. And besides, why haven't I found *you,* if what you told me is true? If there's all these ways to look people up and write to them? Why didn't I just ogle you years ago?"

"*Google,* and I don't know," Jonas said. "But I don't care. Just tell me your last name. "

"Duncan," she said.

Duncan. It was a common name, probably too common. Laura Duncan. What would he find out? He didn't want to know; he didn't want the Internet to know more of his fate than he did, or to be responsible for any more of his life. Hundreds and thousands and millions of sensors, connections, and transmissions that he had no control over. All that meant anything was this moment, right now.

Jonas reached over and held the small of her back against the palm of his hand.

"I know this sounds strange," he said. "I know all of this sounds strange and impossible to believe, but I love you, and that's all that needs to be real."

He kissed her mouth. He opened his heart and let his thoughts, his feelings, his history, dissolve into hers. He felt her lips and her tongue; he felt her teeth and the inside of her soul. He had never wanted anything more than he wanted her. He wanted to fix everything, protect her. Stop time and pull them out.

"I wish there was someplace we could go," Laura said.

"There is," Jonas told her. "But you have to trust me."

She kissed him back, gently, taking his face in her hands. "I do," she whispered. "I will."

"And you can't be afraid of rats."

16

LAURA would not remember the incident itself, only the tension leading up to it. The long, unfruitful day at the crafts fair, the longer car ride back, the owner of the restaurant running after their car with a baseball bat, Mitchell getting sick later, holding his head out the window and throwing up.

It was something Laura said or did as they were walking into the house. But when Bruce hauled off and punched her in the stomach, she went down. It seemed instinctual to curl her body into as small a ball as she could and stay there. She felt what she assumed was his foot kick her in the back, twice. He said *something* to her with each kick, but Laura wouldn't have been able to recount what it was. Everything from her memory was washed away when she looked up, from her odd perspective under the dining-room table, and saw that her mother was standing there the whole time.

She didn't remember much, no, nothing of the incident at all, over the next week. When her mother let her know she'd be going to her dad's in New York the following Friday, Laura packed her stuff into her backpack. She stood outside while Bruce pushed the VW down the driveway as her mother, sitting inside it, popped the clutch and threw the car into gear. Once the car was running, they switched places and Laura quietly got into the backseat.

"Let your father know Mitchell isn't coming." Her mother faced forward while she talked. "Tell him he had band practice or something."

School had been out for a week.

And no one mentioned what had happened to Laura. Not her mother. Not Mitchell. Certainly not Bruce. No one said anything about the punch, the kick, Laura's seeming disassociation with the whole experience. Laura would never really understand how she had provoked Bruce's violence, as if anything could be explained.

What had she done wrong? Left the lights on?

Was the door unlocked? She couldn't remember. She would never remember. The only image imprinted in her mind was her mother's face—and her mother's silence. It would be the last time she ever saw Bruce, and it was the last time she saw or spoke to her mother for a long, long time.

THE rumble of the train started far off, from deep inside the subway tunnel. The pitch of the train got higher as it neared, as if someone were playing an instrument and sliding up a scale. But the sound wasn't really getting higher, was it? It was an illusion, a trick the sensory world played on its inhabitants. Just like the glow inside the subway car when Laura stepped on, turned around, and Jonas was right behind her.

She called out his name, fearing he might be another illusion, light waves passing through time, but here he was, standing next to her, so close she could smell his clothing, the minty scent of his breath. Was he real? And then, as if in response, the subway thrust her forward, and she felt the solidness of his body as he stopped her fall. He was real.

When he wrapped his arms around her, suddenly everything elusive became known, everything shattered became whole, everything harmful became safe. Everything ugly was now beautiful. The world she had left behind slipped away, and the most real thing she could feel was Jonas's strength holding her up as she cried out, a sound that came from a single unbroken spot in her heart.

"What is it?" he asked her. "What's wrong?"

In his arms, time fell away, all the time that had passed for her and not for Jonas. While he held her, there was only the present. She could tell him what had happened, about Bruce, about her mother, about Mitchell, but all of it would be history for him. It would be long since past when he got back home and fell into his own bed.

But when he kissed her, she existed as if she were only just born in this moment. She wanted only to prolong this time, to melt into his body and have him melt into hers. Jonas said he had a plan, somewhere he could take her, somewhere they could be together and be alone. Suddenly nothing else mattered but the union of their time, the union of their memories.

"You have to trust me," Jonas told her, and in that point in time she did. "And you can't be afraid of rats."

"THERE you are. There you are, for Christ's sake. I've been looking all over for you. I need to paint my masterpiece," Max said. "And it needs to be tonight."

Max hopped on the car just before it left Manhattan heading into the Bronx, like crossing a meridian; the train lifted into the air, elevated on the tracks above the streets.

"I need you to promise to do something for me," Max said. He stood in the center of the subway, holding on to the middle pole, letting his body drop left and then right. He was agitated. He had a suitcase with him, presumably filled with spray cans, and a camera bag hanging from his shoulder.

"When? Now?" Jonas asked. Laura sat quietly, holding his hand.

"No, man . . . early in the morning. I mean early, like first-thing early."

"I didn't bring my camera . . ." Jonas started to say.

"Never mind. I have one here. You can't go home tonight," Max said. "I need you."

"We weren't planning to," Jonas said. He felt his face heat up.

Max scooted along the seats and sat down right beside Jonas. He lowered his voice, though the one other guy in the car was fast asleep and looked like he had been for forty years. "I'm going to bomb this train tonight, and when it comes out of the layup, as soon as it hits daylight, as soon as it crosses the El, you've got to get the pictures."

Jonas started to interrupt him, but Max kept talking. "You've got to be there right on 149th Street. It's the best spot, and you can't miss. You can't go back. They'll break up the train as soon as they see it, and then, car by car, they'll buff. You understand?"

Both Jonas and Laura nodded.

"But why don't you just do it?" Laura asked him.

Max pulled the camera strap over his head and off his shoulder. "I can't. Here." He handed the bag to Jonas. "Take this. I've rigged it up with a battery on the advance. I can't be there. They'll be watching. They've got real cops now on the rails, and they'd bust me the minute they saw me. But a white boy with a camera, a white boy that looks like you — they wouldn't know what to make of you."

Jonas took the bag. "You rigged it?"

"Yeah, just hold down the release. Make sure the battery is attached. It will shoot and keep shooting. Just hold your frame steady and get the whole train. Got it? Get the whole train, that's the key."

Jonas poked his head inside the camera bag. "Oh, sure. That's easy. It's got an automatic advance, OK? You rigged it? Yourself? Wow."

"Automatic release. Advance. Whatever you say. You've just got to promise. Time is running out," Max said. "Anyway, I gotta go. I gotta drop this off, get the rest of my paint and my crew, and come back."

Max leaned over and spoke directly into Jonas's ear. Then he bumped him on the shoulder and stood up again. "Hey, it's been real," he said to Laura. "Peace."

When the train stopped, Max jumped off, and he seemed to fade. The night filled in the space around him. The one streetlight on the platform was broken. He was in shadow, barely visible.

"Just promise me," he shouted to Jonas from the platform.

"I promise," Jonas called back.

"We promise," Laura added.

17

JONAS had no intention of not seeing Laura again, even if it meant meeting her on the subway in the middle of the night for the rest of his life; living on a diet of Chinese takeout; raising their children to be careful of the third rail; growing old and dying with nothing but an MTA MetroCard in his pocket. There had to be a way to make this work, to make this right. To make it real, more real. They had to stay on track. It had to work. It just had to.

He had held Laura's hand in the darkness; he watched her steps carefully, and together they climbed back inside the empty subway car. Max had explained exactly how to get inside a car with no electricity, and he had empathically suggested they find a money car, the cleanest by far. Plus, he'd explained, writers don't go for them, because no one ever sees those cars, so the work bums and cops don't bother checking them, because there're no writers to bust. "You'll be alone there, all night," Max had assured them.

The early-summer night brought a coolness, especially in the tunnels. Jonas could feel Laura's skin rise into goose bumps.

"Here." He took off his jacket and slipped it around her shoulders. The money car had no seats, just benches like tables, for counting money, Jonas figured. It was empty, but it kind of looked like a hospital room, with canvas platforms and cabinets. It *was* clean. They lay down on the benches.

Time is a funny thing. The way it lingers and hangs around when you're bored, and the way it moves faster when you need more than is given. Jonas wanted to know every part of Laura's body, touch every inch of her skin, and kiss her so deeply he would devour her and so be vanquished. The union of their bodies, his into hers, and hers engulfing his, brought him to the completion of his existence in a way he had never known before.

And when they were consumed and then completed, when they pulled away from each other but stayed close, it was as if he could feel the minutes and the seconds ticking by, slipping away, taunting him. They rested side by side, his jacket beneath them, their bare legs entwined.

"You can't go back to that house," Jonas told her. He felt her smallness beside him, her femininity, her beauty, and anger grew inside him. "You have to tell your father. And you have to tell him tonight."

Laura was quiet.

"If I could do something, shit, if I could do anything — but I'm stuck. It's crazy. I love you. You can't go back to that house. You have to tell your dad." Jonas tried to sit up, but the bench was too narrow. He put his feet on the floor and stood. "You have to promise me, right here and right now."

Laura started to cry.

"Oh, God. I'm sorry." Jonas got on his knees. "Oh, fuck. I'm so sorry. I didn't mean to upset you. Oh, God. I would never . . ."

"No," Laura told him. "It's not that. I've just never felt like this before. I feel your love," she said. "It's like I can really feel it."

Jonas was so relieved. He smiled. "C'mon. You'll catch a cold. We have to get dressed." Jonas handed Laura her clothes. "You need to tell your dad. Can you promise me?"

"What if he doesn't care?"

Jonas wrapped his arms around her. "Is that

what's stopping you from telling him? Are you afraid he won't do anything about it?"

Laura nodded. "Maybe."

"You can't protect him from the chance to protect you," Jonas told her. "Please promise me you'll tell him."

"That's a lot of promises for one night," Laura said.

Jonas remembered his commitment to Max. "Oh, shit. Right. We have to get up to the El."

They dressed silently, shyly, and made their way out of the car, holding hands.

The sun was rising outside; tiny slivers of light made their way through cracks in the ceiling and the dusty grate above. The trains would leave the yard by six thirty in the morning. It had to be nearly that now.

Jonas gathered Max's camera equipment, and took Laura's hand. "Look, if we get out there and we're all alone again, if one of us disappears, or we both do, we'll meet back at the station. I'll be there every Saturday night until you show up. OK? OK?"

They stepped out onto the platform between the cars and headed back through the tunnel.

"He'll make me live with him," Laura said. "My dad. He'll make me leave there."

Morning was making itself known, the closer they got to the fencing. They would have to climb up and make their way across the platform. They could hear voices in the distance, the conductors checking their cars.

"I know," Jonas said. "That's what I'm counting on." He boosted her up.

"You'll really wait for me?" Laura asked. She looked down toward him.

"Laura," Jonas said. "Look, no matter what happens, you have to take care of yourself. *I* don't matter, and *we* don't even matter. You matter to me and you have to matter to yourself. Promise me you'll tell him about Bruce. And then we'll meet again at the station when you get back. At Fifty-ninth."

"I will. I love you," she said.

"I know. I feel your love," he told her. "I can actually feel it."

It would bring them together again. He was certain of it.

A tripod would have helped immensely, Jonas thought as he set up the camera. He made a makeshift stand out of a cardboard box and a piece of wood that he found on the platform. He checked the light and the film. With a few tester shots, he made sure the battery was attached and working. Just as Max had predicted, the train came out of the tunnel. It was magnificent, like a magical dragon from a fiery pit. The burner, Max's piece, was five cars of a twelve-car train; the entire surface of all five cars, including the windows, was backwashed in baby blue, like a perfect summer sky, and dotted with white clouds so light and puffy they looked like the whole train might melt into the sky. The *M* was outlined in black, so deep and solid it seemed to be cut right into the steel of the train, and it was filled with green fading into orange into yellow. The *A* was the same, followed by the *X*. MAX. He had used his real name. Off to the right side, mostly on the fifth car, he had painted a three-dimensional tear, with cracks stemming from the edges, as if the whole train were about to break into pieces.

Know how to live with the time that is given you, was written in luminous deep purple coming from inside the three-dimensional painted crack.

Jonas turned to say something to Laura, to grab her around the waist and laugh with her, but he knew she was already gone. He had lost sight of her as soon as they pulled themselves from the tracks and touched the pavement.

The camera clicked away — thirty-six shots in fifteen seconds — capturing the whole train, frame by frame. Steel had turned to sky. The masterpiece flew across the top of the city. Jonas imagined a crowd gathered on the platform, early-morning commuters on their way into the city. He could see businessmen, nurses, teachers, cleaning women, kids on their way to school. He could almost hear one person clapping, then another, and another, until everyone on the platform was applauding. Even below, down on the street, people stopped what they were doing, stopped their conversations, stopped their cars, to witness this incredible piece of art, this majesty of style, before it rushed by and was gone.

"Toss it to me!"

"What the hell—?" Jonas spun around.

"Toss it to me, just the film," Max said. "Not the camera. They'll notice the camera."

"Who?" Jonas asked.

"Just toss it!"

Jonas wound the film in the camera until it was safely back inside its cassette, then opened up the back of the camera and tipped it out. He tossed the film over to Max.

"I can develop it," Jonas told him.

"So can I," Max said. He was moving fast. "But, hey, thanks, man. I owe you one."

18

NICK had tried for two full months to get his friend to come out on a Saturday night. He'd even agreed to hang out on the subway with him a few times. One Saturday they rode back and forth on the 4, 5, and 6 trains until two in the morning. Now Nick was following Jonas down his block.

"I'm organizing an intervention. Just thought I'd tell you," Nick said.

"I thought you weren't supposed to tell the person. I thought the element of surprise was an important part of an intervention." Jonas untwisted the leashes, hand under hand, when the two dogs stopped to sniff at the same trash cans. "Is that why you're stalking me?"

"Well, it's not officially organized yet," Nick answered. "And I'm not stalking you. I'm coming along for the ride . . . or the walk, as the case may be."

Jonas made twenty bucks a day per dog whenever someone in his building went away and wanted his services.

"Maybe you want to weigh in during the planning stage," Nick said.

"Don't worry so much about me." Jonas stopped when the dogs stopped. He reached in his pocket for his plastic scooper bags, but the dogs kept walking. "False alarm."

Nick followed. "I'm not so much worried about you as terrified. You can't keep waiting for her. She either isn't coming or never did."

Jonas stopped. "You still think I'm crazy."

"Kind of. Maybe it's all the weed."

Not likely.

All four stopped at the corner, waiting for the light to change. Casper, a whitish Shar-Pei–Lab mix sat down on the curb; as soon as he did that, Jengo, an overweight boxer, sat down next to him.

"Oh, crap. They hate to move. C'mon, guys. Let's go." The white walk light came on.

"I'm not crazy, Nick, but I don't know. It's so long ago, I'm forgetting. Maybe you're right."

An older woman with a severe face-lift rushed up from behind with her dog, some kind of poodle, and passed by. As if on cue, both Casper and Jengo got up and started walking again.

"Look, I tried searching everything. Google, WhitePages. I plugged every spelling of her name, first and last, into Facebook and Classmates.com and whatever that Linked-on thing is. There's nothing. Or nothing that's her. Nothing that fits."

Nick listened. They were almost at the dog park on Riverside. "Well, did you try that microfiche or microfilm at the public library?"

"What's that?"

"You know, those rolls of teeny, tiny print from, like, a hundred years ago—records and documents and newspapers from everywhere. You have to go downstairs and use this huge machine, but I think it's got stuff that never made it onto the Internet."

"No," Jonas said. "Should I?"

"If you want to find out once and for all. . . . I mean, I think maybe this is a way." Nick slowed his steps and his voice. "I mean, I don't get any of this, Jonas. But if you can find some peace, I really wish you would, and if I can help, I will."

"Thanks," Jonas said. He unfastened the leashes inside the fenced-in area, and they watched both dogs bound off about four or five feet with their new and sudden freedom, then sit back down in the grass and wait.

⊡⊡⊡

"YOU'RE going to the library?"

"Is that so strange?" Jonas didn't feel like explaining, not to his mother.

"You don't have to be nasty. Just a straight answer would do. It's not too much to ask for. I'm not trying to control you, just be a part of your life."

Jonas didn't answer, though he thought his mother had had a little more *oomph* lately, and that was a good thing. He grabbed his backpack, the one he hadn't used since middle school but found in the bottom of his closet, his camera bag, and his keys.

"Sorry, Mom." He stood at the door. "I've just got to do something, and I don't feel like talking about it."

"Well, at least that sounds honest," she said. She smiled, which made Jonas feel worse. He should have understood how she felt about anything that sounded cryptic or secretive. He had been both, for quite a few months.

"I'll be back by dinner," he told her. He leaned in

and kissed her on the cheek, something he hadn't felt like doing for a long time. "Tell Lily I'll pick up some good books for her."

Jonas's mother looked like she was going to cry. "That would be real nice," she said, and Jonas slipped out the door, into the hall.

"That's downstairs," the librarian informed him. "You do have a current New York Public Library card?"

Jonas thought about lying, but that didn't make much sense if he needed it to access the microfilm. Playing dumb was the next best thing.

"Uh, no, actually. Do I need one?"

The librarian didn't appear to be buying his act or didn't care. "You can use a temporary card for today or maybe you'd like to get a real library card. We still have some things here you can't get online."

"I'm counting on just that."

Another librarian showed Jonas how to search for microfilm and how to load the microfilm reader.

"You can search a town, but you might want to narrow down the year and probably the month. You said you were doing research on the nineteen seventies in upstate New York? What part?"

"Woodstock." Jonas figured there was no harm in answering.

The librarian laughed. "Well, that's not exactly

upstate. Have you looked at a map of New York State lately?"

Jonas didn't like this woman at all.

"Are you researching the music festival?"

Some librarian; she didn't even know Woodstock wasn't at Woodstock.

"Because then you'd need to go to Bethel, New York," she went on. Jonas really wanted her to leave him alone.

"I got it," Jonas told her. "Thanks." He felt his phone buzz in his pocket.

"I'm over there if you need me." She looked back. "And please, no cell phones."

He decided not to ask her if texting was allowed; he was going to do it anyway. It was Nick, asking where he was.

Library.
　　Which one?
The one with the lions.
　　The *Ghostbuster* one?
Yeah.
　　I'll be right over.

And Jonas began to sift through the tiny rolls of film, scrolling them one by one through the light machine that read the film and projected it into a private viewing box. It was completely different from surfing the Net. You couldn't search a particular word; you had to scan the whole document with your eyes, side to side, up and down. Jonas wasn't even sure what he was looking for.

Notices, property records, announcements, any newspaper article that might mention Laura or anyone in her family. He wished he had asked her more questions, anything. Her father's first name, her mother's maiden name, you know, all the regular information you get when you're getting to know someone.

This was impossible.

It was near noon when Nick showed up.

"How did you find me?" Jonas asked, rubbing his eyes.

"You're the only one down here under forty-five," Nick said.

Jonas looked around. That wasn't exactly true; there were some people who looked like grad students, but mostly there were professor types and older people at the other machines.

"How's it going?"

"Not so good," Jonas told him. Several heads were raised in disapproval. Jonas lowered his voice. "But I'm only up to Woodstock, April nineteen seventy."

"Are you going through every year?"

Jonas nodded. "Well, it's a weekly paper, and yeah,

I thought I'd start in nineteen sixty-nine and work my way up."

Nick pulled out his wallet. "Well, I'll start down, then, and we'll meet in the middle."

"You have a library card?"

"Screw you, Goldman. I'll be right back."

For the next ten minutes they worked quietly. "What year did she think it . . . *say* it was?" Nick asked.

"Nineteen seventy-three. July, same month as now," Jonas answered. He was sifting mechanically through articles, police blotters, obituaries, wedding announcements, and even advertisements. He remembered Laura mentioning a store her mom worked at stringing beads. And all the while, he was hoping she had left Woodstock and was living with her dad. New York City would be harder to search — he had already discovered there were over two hundred and fifty people in New York with the surname Duncan — but that would be next.

"What if we do find something?" Nick leaned over and whispered. "I mean, isn't that kind of creepy? I don't even want to think of all the possibilities, but like . . ." And then he stopped.

"What?" Jonas said. "What? What do you see? What did you find?"

"You said her name was Laura Duncan and she had a brother, Mitchell?"

Jonas nearly tipped over his chair, climbing out and looking into Nick's screen. Heads popped up all over, but Jonas didn't care. He looked down into the microfilm projector, and there it was, a small notice, in the *Woodstock Village News,* July 23, 1973:

Tragically, Laura Duncan, of New York City, was killed by a motor car that jumped the sidewalk while she was traveling abroad with her father, Henry Duncan, also of New York City. She is survived by a brother, Mitchell Duncan, and her mother, Janis Duncan, both residing in Woodstock, New York. There will be a private memorial service. No other information has been given at this time.

"Oh, man," Nick let out. "I am so sorry. Oh, God. Oh, Jonas, I'm so sorry. Hey, wait for me."

By the time Nick cleaned everything up, returned the film, and signed them both out of the machines, Jonas was nowhere to be found.

LAURA wished she could have killed off Mitchell too, but the way she explained it to Zan, it was just easier this way. Oddly, Zan didn't question any of it at all. She only said she was going to miss Laura after she moved to New York City with her dad, but agreed that it was the best thing.

We can stay best friends, Laura said. We can talk on the phone and you can visit. They hugged and promised, but of course it didn't happen that way.

Laura also hoped that after she talked to her dad about Bruce, nobody would bother her much about the fake notice in the paper. Heck, they might not even see the obituary she had called into the *Woodstock Village News*.

It was much easier to do than Laura had anticipated, but on another level much harder.

"Can you spell that, please?" the woman on the phone asked. She sounded busy and as if she were making a huge effort to sound sympathetic. Laura wanted to let her know there was no need to pretend to care, since no one had really died, but that would have defeated the whole purpose, of course.

"*D-u-n-c-a-n.* Henry, of New York City."

"Yes, I got that part. And there's no funeral information? No place to send donations? Flowers? Cards?"

Laura hadn't thought of that when she made the call. "Uh, no. It's private. The family is very private."

"OK, then. You will see it in next week's obits. I am sorry for your loss," the woman said.

"Thank you very much." Laura hung up and then it was hard. It was like a piece of her very soul had been torn out of her body. The very thing that could make her whole, that had filled her heart and given her meaning, she had just thrown away. There was no worse feeling, because it was her choice. It would be like a starving person denying herself food and feeling herself die. She was dying, and yet they were both just beginning to live.

They had to live.

It was as if imagining the impossible — like being in the Holocaust and choosing not to be liberated — because Laura knew she had to let Jonas go and she wanted to believe there truly was another world to come, where they would be together.

Laura decided to tell her father everything on her next visit, although she made sure not to take the subway.

"Well, I'm not walking," Mitchell told his sister. He had gone with her this time, as it had been three months since he had been to the city and their dad was leaving for Europe in a few weeks.

"Suit yourself," Laura said. She turned to see Mitchell fall into step beside her. "I'm going to tell dad I want to live with him."

They walked together up Eighth Avenue. When

they got to the next corner, Mitchell put out his hand to stop her from crossing. The light was about to turn red. It was almost like old times.

"That's probably better," he said.

Laura looked at his face. He looked sad, confused, maybe. He wasn't all that much older than she was. Everyone has to figure out their own way to survive.

"You could lie and tell me you'll miss me," Laura said. The light changed and brother and sister stepped down off the curb.

"As a matter of fact, I will," Mitchell said.

HARDEST of all was telling her father. He looked sick and then angry and then sick again and then guilty as hell, and then he looked like he was going to cry, which was the worst thing of all. When Laura saw her father's pain, she nearly regretted telling him about Bruce. She would rather have continued living in Woodstock than have brought this anguish to her dad.

You can't protect him from the chance to protect you.

But Laura wasn't so sure. In that moment, it seemed more frightening to see her father so defeated, but it was too late.

And in the end, nothing so horrible happened. Her dad drove to Woodstock and picked up her things. He got her bed, her desk and chair, her chest of drawers, and most of her belongings. There were a few things he left behind, because he didn't know they belonged to her. Laura didn't want to see Bruce ever again, and not even her mother for a long time.

TO tell the truth, Laura didn't see or talk to her mother again until she herself was thirty-eight years old and received her cancer diagnosis, malignant neoplasm of the breast documented as carcinoma. Her mother drove across the country, from her home in Salt Lake City. Bruce was long gone. No one knew anything of what had become of him. Laura had spent some time in her early twenties trying to track him down, considering maybe confronting him, punching him in the face with her fist. But after a while it didn't seem important anymore. Just as she knew she had to move on and live her life without Jonas, at some point she let finding Bruce go. She could finally store all those bad memories in another part of her mind, where they couldn't hurt her anymore and they became just memories. And slowly, over time — not at first, and not for a long while, but eventually — she began to forget about Jonas as well. She went to the High School of Art and Design and then to RISD to study graphic art, always partial to urban art forms. Whenever the girls at school started talking about boys, about sex and love, Laura would think of a dream she had, a long time ago, and it made her smile.

Mitchell lived nearby in New Rochelle, running a software company out of his home. He had three children. Laura fell in love and married Bobby Rabinowitz, and they were together for twelve years. They had no children of their own, but Bobby had two young sons from a previous marriage, and when Laura died, in 1996, they cried for her as they would have for their own mother.

19

JONAS stopped waiting for her, but he never stopped keeping his eyes open. He took the subway more often than he probably needed to.

"Jonas, you're not eating much these days," his mother said. "Is it the heat?" She knew it wasn't — heat had certainly never slowed down his appetite before — but it was nice of her to throw that in there in case he still didn't want to talk about it.

It had been a horrible end to the summer, with record-breaking heat waves. Everyone was talking about global warming, along with all the other horrors of the modern world: Internet predators, identity theft, homegrown terrorism, AIDS, mad cow disease.

Sometimes his heart ached so badly he tried to tell himself Laura was better off not living in this time.

"It's not the heat," Jonas told his mother, which was pretty much the same as saying *Yes, Mom. Something's really wrong and I want to talk about it, but I think talking to you would be the world's worst idea because you always overreact, make it about you, or, in this case, wouldn't believe me anyway.*

His mother stayed quiet.

"Where's Lily?" Jonas asked. He took another bite of his chicken and then pushed his plate away.

"She's at Beatrice's house. Isn't that a funny name for a little girl? I haven't heard that name since I was a kid."

Laura would never change in his mind, but of course, if she had lived, she would be his mother's age or close to it. It would never have been possible; he knew that and he took some small solace in knowing she had gotten away from Bruce in the end. She was referred to as living in New York City. She must have moved in with her dad. They must have been on vacation together. He hoped she was having a good time and that she felt safe before . . .

"I'm not doing so well, Ma," Jonas began.

She didn't jump in. She didn't even look too interested, so Jonas found the courage to go on. "I, well, I lost someone. Someone I loved. Really loved. And it's not just that she's gone but that it would never have worked out anyway, but I would have done anything to make it work. I feel like . . . I feel like . . . I feel like I would have . . ."

"Died to keep her?" his mother asked.

"Yeah."

Of course, she understood. That's how she felt when his dad left. Why she lay in bed all morning, all weekend, coming out only to fix dinner, or more likely order it in. He shouldn't have gone here. He regretted saying anything.

"Maybe she was your *beshert*."

Jonas looked up. "Was dad your *beshert*?"

"Yes, I think he was. I think he still is, but he got lost. Did your girl get lost?"

He didn't want to cry. The last thing he wanted to do was cry, but his throat stung and burned. Laura got lost. They were both lost from the start.

"She'll be back, then." Jonas's mother began to clear the dishes. She had a peacefulness about her. Maybe it had been coming on for a while, but Jonas was only now noticing.

"What do you mean?"

She didn't sit back down, and Jonas was grateful. She moved easily from the table to the kitchen counter, closing the ketchup, wiping down their plates. "Well, if you don't find your *beshert* on earth, or if you meet each other but, for one reason or another, you fail to connect . . ." Her voice faltered but then she regained her strength. "Or if for some reason you connect but then one of you forgets, you get another chance."

"Another chance?" His mother was sounding a lot like Morah Frieda from Hebrew school, but it was comforting in an odd way.

"You are reborn," she told Jonas. "At least, that's what the kabbalists say. Your soul will return to earth to find its mate. When two people are destined in heaven to be together, they are complete, and the repairing of the world can begin."

"You believe that?" Jonas asked his mother.

She sat down across the table from her son. "I don't know, Jonas. I know I loved your father and always will. I know we made two beautiful children together, and that's my *haolam habah,* the world to come. And will we meet again in another life? Well, I truly hope so."

It seemed so sad, so terribly, wretchedly sad, and Jonas wanted to tell her everything. He wanted to say how sorry he was for breaking her heart, now that he had one of his own. How sorry he was for ruining her life.

"You know, Jonas, you should probably know something else," his mother began. He didn't like the sound of that, but at this point, he didn't have much more to lose.

"What?"

"I knew about your father. I knew it all—way before I found those e-mails in your room."

Now it was Jonas's turn to stay quiet.

"In a way, it was the best thing that could have happened. It was like shining a light on a hidden shame, and then it forces you to look at yourself. If you hadn't done that, I might have gone on pretending."

"Maybe that would have been better."

"No, it's never better. And it wasn't the first time, or the first woman. So I should thank you for humiliating me once and for all." She laughed. She actually laughed.

"And in the meantime, there's JDate." His mother bounced up.

"Hey, Mom. Did you lose weight?"

She popped him lightly on the head with her dish towel. "It's about time you noticed."

HE tried to tell the boy; he tried to tell Jonas that she wasn't coming back. She wasn't ever coming back. It was crazy to watch him waiting like that, hanging around the subway stations and platforms. Then one night, when Max was working on a piece at the 149th Street layup, he thought he saw her. It was her, he was certain. What the hell was she doing up here?

"Laura?" he called down the tunnel. His voice echoed, but no other sound returned. She was around; he knew it. But she wasn't coming back. The rift shifted. The universe repaired itself. Someone needed to document, to bear witness. That's what the artists are for.

"You know what *real* crazy is? You know what's really crazy?" Max talked out loud while he mapped out his idea with a marker. "Crazy is doing all this work, making my art, putting all my heart and soul into this shit, knowing it's probably not going to last the week."

Max uncapped his cans and lined them up on the floor in the order that he would need them: Blue Ocean Breeze, Tangerine Orange, Cherry Red, Almond, Smoky Gray. Then he climbed up, grabbing the bar that ran across the top of the train, and dangling from one arm, he sprayed the outline that would appear above the windows. He jumped down and continued the line, unbroken, right across the glass and down to the bottom of the car.

IT was a full year, or more, before Jonas could ride the subway without scanning every person, every face, every girl in the car, every time. He had hooked up a few times with a girl from his American history class. And once with another girl from health, and he didn't even realize he had stopped looking until he saw her.

She was the tiniest bit shorter and had reddish hair, not dark brown. About his age, fifteen, maybe sixteen, years old. She was wearing a vintage shearling coat and a long scarf. It was Christmas season in New York; the city was crowded, the subways packed with too many people and way too many packages. Jonas watched her get on, and when she got up to leave at Grand Central, he followed her off.

It was crazy, and his heart was beating hard. He wove in and out of the hordes of people, trying to stay close to her but not stalkerish close. She was walking like she didn't quite know where she was going, like maybe she was from out of town. But she made her way through the underground walkway and then up to the train station.

There was a huge crafts fair going on in the lobby, just like there was every year in Grand Central, real high-end stuff, overpriced but fun to walk through. The arch that stretched over the whole event was decorated with tiny white lights and garlands. The items must have been too expensive for the girl, because she wandered up and down, touching things, talking to the vendors, but didn't buy anything. Jonas made sure to stay far enough away, but every now and then he caught a piece of her voice.

"This hat would look perfect on you," one of the vendors was saying. "It's totally throwback. Couldn't you just see this on Janis Joplin?"

"Or Stevie Nicks," the girl said. She held the hat and looked it over in her hands. Jonas stepped closer.

"What do you think?" She popped it on her head and turned to look right at him.

"Me?" For a second he froze. Maybe she knew he had been following her, but she didn't seem worried. She just looked happy and flirty, adorable.

"Well, sure, you. What do you think?"

Lots of girls look great from behind, but then they turn around. Jonas always said that, though Nick wouldn't agree. For Jonas, it was the face that mattered most. This girl had looked great from behind, and Jonas had had a long time to notice. Now she was looking right at him. Now he could see her skin and her eyes, her cheeks, her smile.

And she was beautiful. She put her hand up to twist a piece of her hair between her thumb and ring finger. It was a gesture he couldn't mistake. It was so familiar, his heart ached, his heart broke, his heart soared.

EPILOGUE

Graffiti art has all but disappeared from the New York scene. In the 1980s, subway art became associated with crime. Crack was becoming an epidemic in cities all over the country. In 1984, the New York City Transit Authority (NYCTA) began a five-year program to eradicate graffiti. At the same time that it was disappearing, graffiti had begun to enter the contemporary art world, and, though it was still controversial, many people considered it a legitimate form of expression. Some of the better-known street artists actually went on to become reputable commercial artists and muralists.

In May 2013, the Portia Gallery on Spring Street mounted a retrospective called Art of the Underground, collecting the very few extant photographs depicting the graffiti-covered trains and some very rare shots of the artists themselves. The gallery owner, David Lowery, had gone to considerable lengths and expense to enlarge one photo in particular. It was a single long, continuous shot of a burner, an entire train, coming across the El in what looks to be the South Bronx. The lighting and composition are exquisite. The early-morning light can be seen illuminating the brilliant colors, so that the train appears to shine from the print. There is some disagreement as to who took the photo, or how it was done. According to anyone who is knowledgeable about the subject, photographic technology enabling such a crystal-clear panoramic shot of a moving train had not yet been made available to the general public. But everyone who saw the photograph had to admire it, stop a moment, pause, and take in the purple message: *Know how to live with the time that is given you.*

ACKNOWLEDGMENTS

With incredible gratitude to:

Nancy Gallt, Marietta Zacker, Deb Noyes, Pam Marshall, Hannah Mahoney, and Ann Stott. The writing life might be solitary, but a book is the effort of many talents.

And to all those who kept me alive this past year, you know who you are.

And to Steve, Sam, and Ben.